THE OPERATION

A steel blade glistened in the orange light before me.

A gloved hand pressed it on to the top of my skull.

This I could feel – the metal teeth fastening into my skin.

They began to saw. The noise. The blood.

The sorrow of it all.

Yet my eyes – they must have left those intact. I watched as the eye of the computer screen took me deeper into my brain, even as the indifferent fingers probed the underlying layers of my grey tissue. Here, it was also dark. No synapses with shooting molecular bolts of lightning. Not a single neuron glowed with the memory of days spent beneath the sun. The pathways of consciousness were as silent as my pleas for help. Yet there was life, yet not life as I knew it.

Not life as God had created it at the beginning of time.

I saw a flash of silver. It was horrible. It was the seed of the curse – that I knew for a fact, even if the shadows did not. Yet it was also brilliant. The seed could reveal the secrets of the universe.

It was my destiny to know them all.

ABOUT THE AUTHOR

Christopher Pike was born in New York, but grew up in Los Angeles, where he lives to this day. Prior to becoming a writer, he worked in a factory, painted houses and programmed computers. His hobbies include astronomy, meditating, running and making sure his books are prominently displayed in his local bookshop. He is the author of the best-selling CHAIN LETTER, SPELLBOUND, LAST ACT, GIMME A KISS, WEEKEND, SLUMBER PARTY, REMEMBER ME, the FINAL FRIENDS trilogy, SCAVENGER HUNT, FALL INTO DARKNESS, WITCH, SEE YOU LATER, CHAIN LETTER 2, DIE SOFTLY, BURY ME DEEP, MONSTER, ROAD TO NOWHERE, SATI, WHISPER OF DEATH and MASTER OF MURDER which are all available in paperback from Hodder and Stoughton.

CHRISTOPHER PIKE

THE Eternal ENEMY

Hodder & Stoughton

LONDON SYDNEY AUCKLAND

First published in the USA in 1992
by Archway Paperbacks, a division of
Simon and Schuster.

First published in Great Britain in 1993
by Hodder and Stoughton Ltd

British Library C.I.P.

A catalogue record for this book is
available from the British Library

ISBN 0-340-60698-3

Printed and bound in Great Britain
for Hodder and Stoughton Children's
Books, a division of Hodder and
Stoughton Ltd., Mill Road, Dunton
Green, Sevenoaks, Kent TN13 2YA.
(Editorial Office: 47 Bedford Square,
London WC1B 3DP) by Cox & Wyman
Ltd, Reading, Berks.
Typeset by Phoenix Typesetting,
Ilkley, West Yorkshire.

For Paul

ONE

I was just a normal teenage girl. I loved beautiful clothes and loud music, long telephone conversations and sleepy summer evenings. Most of all I loved cookies and boys. My favourite cookies were chocolate chip – with milk. You've got to have milk to have cookies. That's what I always said.

My favourite boys – well, actually, I had only one favourite. His name was Christopher. My name is Rela. I just used to have to think 'Chris and Rela' to get goosebumps – hoping that we would one day be together. Now when I think of us I feel a lot different – sad, very sad. But there is beauty in sorrow. I realise that now. Someone I knew well once said if there was no sorrow in the world there would be no compassion. That's how I feel as I begin this tale – filled with love for all the people of the world.

My people.

How fragile we all are. Time has a permanent hold on us the moment we're born. It allows us to grow to get big. We go to school, we find jobs, we fall in love, get married and have children. Time lets us do all these things. But then, in the end, it kills us. Time is like a friend but only for a time. You see, I don't have a lot of time to tell this story – my old friend has come for me. This time it's my time.

I will begin, then.

7

I wanted to buy a VCR. My father didn't own one. We had to be the only family in Los Angeles that didn't have a machine, and the lack was particularly distressing to me because I loved movies so much. Honestly, on a Saturday or Sunday I could go to three movies in a row and not get tired. I had no taste and could watch anything, even low-budget sci-fi-films with no story and cheesy special effects. Anything sci-fi sent me straight to technological heaven – as long as I had popcorn. Ah, cookies, boys, movies and popcorn. What a life!

Anyway, I wanted to buy a VCR, but I had only two hundred bucks to spend. I had saved the money from my after-school job at our local library – three to nine Monday, Wednesday and Friday. Friends at school had told me Circuit City had good prices and a wide selection, so I went there. It was Thursday afternoon and I had just got out of my art class, where I had been working on a brilliant sculpture of my own head. What vanity, I know, but I was having fun.

A handsome young salesman practically jumped me when I entered the store. I didn't mind because I needed advice on what to buy. The guy was blond and tanned, with bulging muscles that looked like they'd been injected. He was about twenty easy-California-living years old.

'Can I help you?' he asked.

'Yeah,' I said. 'I want to buy a VCR.'

He gestured to a shelf of VCR's over his shoulder. A glance at the prices made me nervous – nothing under three hundred. 'We've got a wide selection,' he said. 'Do you know what you're looking for?'

'Something good and cheap.'

He was amused. 'How cheap?'

'Two hundred bucks.'

8

'You're going to have to spend more than that to get something good.'

'It's all I've got.'

'Do you have plastic?'

'A credit card?'

'Yes.'

'No,' I said. 'I only have a leather purse with ten twenties in it. That's all I've got in all the world.'

He chuckled. 'Another one of our poor homeless. We get them all the time wanting to buy sophisticated electronic equipment.' He turned. 'Let's find you a VCR you like – then you can worry about paying for it.'

In the next five minutes Ed – he had on a name tag – explained why he preferred certain brands over others, and why two hundred bucks wasn't going to cut it. Yet as we wandered down the aisle I spotted a couple of machines on sale for less than two hundred. Ed said I didn't want one of them because they had only two heads and I wanted four.

'With only two heads you have horrible quality when you switch to slow motion,' Ed said

'Why would I ever switch to slow motion?' I asked. 'I just want to be able to rent movies and watch them.'

'Have you seen *Lethal Weapon*? The first one?'

'I don't think so.'

'You must have seen it. When it came out on video it was the hottest movie in the country among women. The reason is because there's a scene near the beginning where Mel Gibson walks across the room, butt naked. Now, you've got to have slow motion to enjoy that scene fully. If you have only two heads on your VCR and you watch that movie you'll probably break your blasted machine.'

I must have looked somewhat incredulous. 'I'm not

going to risk ruining my VCR just to look at Mel Gibson's butt,' I said.

'What's your name?' Ed asked suddenly.

'Rela.'

'What kind of name is that?'

'A beautiful one. What kind of name is Ed?'

'How old are you?'

'Eighteen. Do I need a licence to operate all four heads?'

He laughed. 'It depends on what you're trying to slow down with all those heads. Look, I like you, Rela, I want to give you a deal. If you spend a little more than you want you'll thank me later.'

I appraised him closely. 'When am I going to see you later, Ed?'

That caught him by surprise. He took a step back and scratched his head through his short hair. 'Well, I wouldn't mind seeing you later, Rela. What's your number?'

'Are you asking me out?'

'Yeah. You sound surprised.'

'I am.'

'Why?'

'You hardly know me. You just met me.'

Ed shrugged. 'I hardly know any of my customers. In fact, I prefer it that way. But you're cute. What are you doing Saturday night?'

'I'm having a party at my house. That's why I want to buy the VCR – so I can show a couple of movies.' I paused. 'But you can't come to the party.'

'Why not?'

I hesitated. 'My boyfriend's going to be there.'

'You have a boyfriend?'

'Yeah. Now you sound surprised.'

'I'm not, actually. I told you, you're cute. I do

want to go out with you. Maybe Sunday night.'

'But—'

'How long have you known your boyfriend?'

'Not long. Actually, he's just a guy I like a lot.'

Ed waved his hand. 'He sounds like a jerk. Let's go to a movie Sunday night. That way you won't have to rent one.'

I stopped and shook my head. 'It's too bad I don't have four heads on top of my shoulders, then maybe I could keep up with you. Let's get back to business, Ed. You were going to give me a deal, and get me to pay more than I want to. How does this all work?'

'Do you have a bank account?'

'Yes, but that's where I got the two hundred in my purse now. I only have ten dollars left in my account.'

Ed wasn't worried. 'You can write us a postdated cheque. I'll tell the manager I know you and that you're trustworthy.' He reached out and put his hand on a black VCR. 'This is a Pioneer. It's pretty popular, and I sell a lot of them. You get four heads – the machine's easy to programme, and Pioneers seldom break down. Normally we sell this model for three hundred and forty, but I can give it to you for two eighty.'

'Do I get such a big discount because you want to go out with me?'

Ed grinned. He wasn't a bad sort. 'You get it because you have a beautiful name, Rela. That's reason enough.'

I bought the VCR. I didn't have to make good on my postdated cheque for sixty days. I figured I'd be ahead of things by then. Ed asked me for my phone number as I was leaving the store. I just laughed. That can be the safest response sometimes.

I didn't laugh when he asked me for my driver's licence so he could write the number down on the back of the cheque. I knew it was his job to ask. I lowered my head and told him I didn't have it with me. He said fine.

I was happy driving home with my new toy beside me on the front seat. I kept looking at it, thinking of all the movies I was going to be able to watch. Next, I thought, I was going to have to buy an electric popcorn popper.

And get a boyfriend.

I knew I had to call Christopher when I got home to invite him to my party. I had to give him some notice so he wouldn't make other plans. But I was too nervous to call right away so I decided to dial my best friend, Stacy, instead.

I had known Stacy for three months, since mid July, when I came to Los Angeles to be with my father. I met her at a park. I went there to fly a kite, or rather to try to fly a kite. There wasn't much wind that day and all my running up and down on the parched lawn wasn't getting my red paper diamond up into the sky. The day was hot and I was sweating gallons. I think Stacy must have watched me for a while before approaching me and asking if I was out of my mind. It was a novel way to say hello, and I liked her right away for it.

Stacy was one of those people who had no time lag between her brain and her tongue. She said exactly what was on her mind. Some people thought she was rude; they didn't know how sensitive she was. Yet, for all her straightforwardness, her wit was subtle – you had to be quick to catch it.

Stacy was big-boned and had short shiny brown hair. She was always making fun of herself. Truly, though, she didn't do this to cover some unseen pain. Stacy was one of the happiest people I knew. She was eighteen – like me. The day I met her she took in my situation, cut my kite tail in half, and had my kite flying high five minutes later.

It was four in the afternoon when I spoke to Stacy. I hadn't unpacked my VCR yet. She called just as I picked up the phone to dial her.

'Rela,' she said, 'do you walk around with the phone plugged into your belly button? You always get it on the first ring.'

'I'm telepathic.' I said. 'I always know when you're thinking of me. Hey, I did it, I—'

'You called Chris? Wow!' she interrupted excitedly. Stacy also loved cookies and boys. One of the reasons she was chubby was that she loved doughnuts as well and could down a whole box without a single swallow of milk. She had no lack of boys calling her, though. They felt safe doing so, I suppose, since she went out with anybody who asked. She was a giving soul and by no means a virgin.

'No,' I said. 'I bought a VCR.'

'Oh.' She was disappointed. 'You should call him. It's easier to ask a guy out over the phone cause then he can't see your face. If he says no, you won't have to hide your disappointment.'

'I'm not asking him out. I'm just inviting him to my party. If he wants to go out with me he's going to have to do the asking. Let me tell you about my VCR. It's got four heads—'

'Oh, cool, you have slow motion. I wish we had slow motion. Last week I watched the first *Lethal Weapon* and I wanted to see—'

'Don't say it,' I interrupted. 'It was two hundred and eighty dollars. I had to give the guy a postdated cheque for eighty.'

'He let you? He must really have had the hots for you.'

'He did. He asked me out right there in the store. He wants to come to my party.'

'Did you tell him where and when?'

13

'No. He was covered with bulging muscles. They almost looked fake.'

'If he has your cheque, he has your address,' Stacy observed. Like I said, she was no fool. She went on, 'Did you tell him the party was this Saturday night?'

'I did. If he comes you can have him. Anyway, I can't call Christopher right now.'

'Why not?'

'I'll have a heart attack if he says no.'

'He might say yes.'

'There's only a fifty-fifty chance at best he'll say yes. I don't want to die. I'm scared – God, this is ridiculous. Are you sure he's not seeing anybody?'

Stacy paused. 'Well, I didn't want to tell you this but I have seen him talking to Debbie Rosten at lunch a few days in a row.'

'Debbie Rosten? God, she's a fox. I hate her. Why does he like her?'

'He was just talking to her. That doesn't mean he *likes* her. I talk to my brother's old dog all the time and it stinks.'

'Debbie does not smell like old dog,' I grumbled. 'I'm not going to call him.'

'Rela!'

'Stacy!'

'What?'

'Nothing. I've got to go. My dad's going to be home in an hour and I want to fix him a feast.'

Stacy laughed. 'You have to ask Chris out tomorrow at school. You won't have any peace until you do.'

'I suppose.'

'What are you going to make for your dad?'

'I don't know – something good.'

'You never told me where you learned to cook.'

'It's just something I picked up over the years,' I said.

*

There were two TVs in our house, one in the living room, the other in my bedroom. When I bought the VCR I intended to put it in the living room so that my dad could enjoy it too. I took it out of the box in my bedroom, though, because I wanted to have privacy while I learned to use it.

I read the instruction manual while I darted between my bedroom and the kitchen. There was fish in the freezer – I decided to cook that instead of the pasta I had been planning. The VCR instruction booklet was easy to follow. Technology was really dancing forward, I thought, as I set the machine to record a movie that was supposed to be HBO late Friday night – actually, super-early Saturday morning – at three AM. Each entry I made flashed on the screen.

The film I was taping was an old sci-fi horror flick that I had seen as a kid. It was called *It! The Terror from Beyond Space! It!* was about a space expedition to Mars that had the misfortune of taking aboard an alien monster that had an insatiable craving for human flesh. I remembered how terrified I had been as a kid when several of the crew members were fleeing from the monster and the thing grabbed one of them by the leg. All you heard, while the camera focused on sweat running down the guy's pals' faces was horrible screaming. 'Help me! Please, God, somebody help me!' That movie gave me nightmares for months – I loved it. I figured *It!* would spice up my party if things got dull. Since the movie was to come on at three in the morning, I was thankful there were such things as microchips with memories.

Memories. Later, did I remember making a mistake programming the machine? No, I didn't, I really didn't, even now I don't think I did. It's all a mystery.

15

I left the VCR in my bedroom, for the time being. My father came home at a quarter to six. His name was the Reverend Spencer Lindquist. He wasn't my real father. I was adopted. Spence was the minister at a Methodist church a mile from our house. He was a modern-day saint, and I don't say that just because he took care of me. He worked with the homeless. He spent hours every day trying to find places for them to sleep. He had also started a successful programme in L.A. called Food For Thought. Leftovers were collected from restaurants and supermarkets and hotels and distributed to the needy. His organisation had half a dozen minivans circulating through all parts of the city. Keeping everything moving and attending to his own church exhausted Spence. He was forty-five but looked ten years older; his hair was already white, and he had a terrible slouch and an irregular heartbeat. But he seemed to thrive on the love and thanks he received from those he helped.

I couldn't have chosen a better father.

'I smell something fishy,' he said as he came into the house. I gave him a big kiss on the cheek, as always. He sat down at the table to eat and I talked about my purchase. I told him the VCR had only cost one hundred and eighty dollars. Of course, I was lying, but I figured it was only a little white lie and that God would forgive me.

How often from that day on did I have to *hope* God would forgive me.

TWO

Dear Chris

I love you, I want you. Do you want me? What? You don't know who I am? I'm the cute brunette who sits two seats behind you on your right in calculus. My eyes are brown, and they light up when I look at you. I can see you right now as I scribble out this note. I wish you would turn to look at me. I really am kind of cute and I don't mean to sound conceited or anything. I'm on the short side but my body is your most wonderful dream. My nose is a button, my smile is a bar of white chocolate. Do you like chocolate, Chris? I like it in cookies. I love you, I think, even though I don't know you. Maybe it's better this way.

No, on second thought, I don't think so. Chris, I feel I have to know you. I feel that if we pass by each other without becoming lovers my life will have been wasted. But I don't want you to think I just want your body. You're brilliant – I want to eat your brains! No, yuck, that's gross. I didn't mean that. I've been watching too many horror films lately. I'm taping one for a party I'm having tomorrow. Would you like to come to my party? The only reason I'm throwing it is so I'll have an excuse to invite you to my house.

Chris, Chris, Chris. I keep thinking your name and thinking that you must be able to hear me thinking and that you must know how much I love you. But how can you know, when I'm afraid to tell you how perfect you are? The moment I first saw you, I silently hid my heart in a golden box to save for you on the day you turned to me and smiled. I wanted you to hold it in your hands. I am so sentimental about you. I'm making myself sick!

Still, I can't help thinking your name, Chris. Christopher Perry. Chris and Rela. I bet you don't even know my last name. I can't remember it myself. Maybe I have the same last name as you. Maybe I will. Rela Perry. I've heard it somewhere before, I swear it.

Let me tell you how I see you. Today you are wearing blue jeans and a white T-shirt. Do you ever wear anything else? I don't mean to be critical. I accept you as you are, but I would love to buy you new clothes to show off your beautiful dark eyes. Do you know I see the night sky when I stare into your eyes? Even from the other side of the courtyard at lunch I can see the moon and the stars in them.

New clothes would also flatter your dark hair, your strong profile. I mainly watch you from the side, you understand because we are not on face-to-face terms yet. What will I say to you when I do finally talk to you? Your mind is so vast, like the ocean. I feel I could drown in it before I could get my bearings. Yeah, I know I also do well in school, but you have imagination. That's the other thing I can see in your eyes, that you will be great, that the world will remember you long after the rest of us have turned to dust. What does a genius need with a girl like me – other than to hold and cuddle and love until the wind comes to blow the dust away . . .

'Rela,' Mr Tudor said.

'Here,' I said, hastily sliding my letter under a piece of scrap paper. I raised my eyes to Mr Tudor, who was standing beside me with our calculus tests in his hand. Two seats up and on my left, Christopher Perry turned to see what was going on. Such an alert face – he had a higher IQ asleep than most of us had awake. He already had his test. He smiled briefly at me and I was momentarily hypnotised.

18

'I know you're here,' Mr Tudor said pleasantly. He laid a test paper on my desk in front of me. 'Catching up on your letter writing?'

Christopher turned back to face front, breaking the spell. 'Yes, sir,' I mumbled. I suspected Mr Tudor had glanced at my letter before he spoke, and maybe he had seen Christopher's name.

'Good luck on your test,' he said. 'Even though you don't need it.'

'Thank you, sir.'

Since I was a straight A student, I was getting an A in calculus. I thought it must have been in my genes – I always did well in maths. The test consisted of six integral problems. I completed them in thirty minutes, about the same time it took for Christopher to finish. I knew I did each one correctly. I sat staring at him while I waited for the class to end. I was slowly marshalling my courage to ask him to my party. Be cool, I kept thinking. Act like it's no big deal, but at the same time make him feel that he's wanted. And above all else, don't burst into tears if he says he's busy.

Mr Tudor finally collected our tests and the bell rang. I gathered up my books and followed Christopher into the hall. He was alone, for the moment, but I knew I had to move fast. I pulled up on his left side, without looking at him. I hoped he'd glance over at me and start a conversation. We were not total strangers. We had talked maybe ten times, probably on an average of five minutes each time. I didn't have to wait long for him to speak.

'The test was a piece of cake, wasn't it?' he said.

I blushed. It was sweet and sentimental of him to speak of cake, which was very sweet, while talking to me.

I knew I had it bad for this guy if I was inventing such comparisons – maybe even to the point of insanity.

'For you, maybe,' I said.

He wasn't fooled. 'You finished sooner than I did, Rela. You always do.'

He said my name, I thought. How auspicious! 'I have to study hard,' I lied. Actually, I never studied. I hardly ever had to look at the textbook. It was enough for me to listen to Mr Tudor.

'What do you have next period?' he asked.

'History, with Palos.'

'Do you like him?'

'He's a nice guy but I think he makes up history as he goes along.'

Christopher raised an eyebrow. 'What makes you say that?'

I didn't know why I had said it – it just seemed true. Often the words that came out of my mouth surprised me. I smiled and shrugged. 'I guess I'm just disappointed that Atlantis and Lemuria aren't discussed in his class.'

Christopher frowned. 'I've heard of Atlantis, but what was Lemuria?'

'Another mythical continent from the past. It was supposed to have been where the Pacific Ocean is now.'

'You must tell me about it some time.' He paused. 'I heard you're having a party Saturday night.'

'Oh?' Ah, heart failure was near. 'Who told you?'

'Stacy. She said it'd be all right if I dropped by, but I wanted to clear it with you first.'

I coughed. 'You can drop by. You can drop by any time you want – that night, I mean. That'd be great.'

'I was wondering if I could bring a friend.'

Oh, my poor heart. Bursting with joy one moment. Just bursting the next. 'Yeah,' I said flatly.

He glanced over at me. 'Are you sure?'

I swallowed thickly. 'Yeah.'

He smiled. 'I've never been to your house. Where do you live?'

His *friend* had devastated me. I couldn't think 'Ask Stacy, she gives the best directions,' I mumbled.

He hesitated. 'I'll do that, Rela. I'll see you there. Is eight o'clock OK?'

'It's OK.'

'Why did you tell him to come when you knew he was bringing a friend?' I yelled at Stacy when I saw her at lunch. We were in the school parking lot. I'd had enough of education for the day – I was going home. That wasn't unusual for me. If I felt like ditching, I ditched. Often I'd drive down to the beach and walk alone along the shore. I loved the wind in my hair, the salt air in my nostrils. The sea always settled my mind. Of course, today there would be no stroll beside the waves. I had to go to work at the library at three.

'He didn't say anything about a friend when I told him about the party,' Stacy said.

'You had no right to tell him about the party in the first place. It was no business of yours.'

'I thought I was doing you a favour. You were so scared, I thought you'd never ask him.'

'I was not scared. I was just waiting for the right moment.'

'I'm sorry.'

I sighed 'Yeah.' I wasn't really mad at Stacy. I was mad at myself for loving someone who obviously didn't love me. It was so frustrating! Why did I care so much about him when I didn't even know him? But that was precisely the point, just what I had written in my letter to him. I did know him. I just didn't know how I knew him. It was cosmic, or else I was losing it.

21

'How do you know his friend is a girl?' Stacy asked. 'Did you ask him?'

'No, I didn't ask him. That wouldn't have been very subtle of me, would it? But he's bringing Debbie, I know it.'

'She's cute,' Stacy observed.

'Shut up.'

Stacy grinned. 'You're giving up without a fight. If he brings her, we'll spill something on her lap. We'll set her on fire. We'll accidentally drown her in the bathtub.'

'We should drown him for bringing her,' I said.

We both laughed at the prospect, but the joke wasn't funny. Indeed, just the idea of Christopher being harmed filled me with inexplicable dread. Of course, that's not a mystery to me now. There were plenty of reasons why I should have worried about him.

And I was one of them.

THREE

The memory of the dream didn't come to me until the next day when I was buying food at the store for my party. I had an orange in my right hand and was squeezing it to see if it was ripe when a strange image flickered inside my mind. The picture itself was suffused with a soft orange glow; perhaps it was the colour of the fruit that triggered the memory. There were objects of other colours in the scene, too. There was a grey reclining chair that reminded me of a dentist's chair because it was surrounded with tubes and pipes. Beside the chair was a squat blue machine that somehow resembled a computer. The chair was partially covered with white sheets, which may have been made of paper. Moving figures flickered at the edge of the scene, but they were hard to distinguish because the orange light shimmered there like fog pierced by the rays of the setting sun. The people – I had to assume they were people – were only clumsy shadows in my mind. They seemed to be carrying something towards the chair; it could have been a person. But as they moved towards the centre of the picture, the whole scene began to fade inside my head.

I blinked and focused on the orange in my hand.

'Wow,' I whispered. Where had those images come from?'

Then I remembered I had not slept well the night before, that I had spent hours tossing and turning and getting up to go to the bathroom when I didn't really have to go. Those same images had been part of a dream I'd had – one that had gone on despite my frequent periods of wakefulness. What surprised me was that I hadn't remembered the dream immediately after I woke up, as I would have expected. But perhaps I had subconsciously blocked it from my memory – temporarily. The dream had been more of a nightmare, I remembered now. A shiver went through me from head to toe. The shadowy figures had been carrying a dead body towards the chair. I put the orange down and steered my cart out of the produce section. I wouldn't have a fruit salad at the party, after all, I decided.

I didn't have time to worry about dreams. I had personally invited four dozen people to my party and God only knew how many others Stacy had asked. I had a list of essentials that I had to buy and my dad's chequebook in my back pocket to pay for them. He had graciously offered to pay for all the food, which was a good thing considering that I had spent every penny I had on the VCR. I hadn't checked to see if the VCR had taped my horror movie, but I assumed that it had.

At the top of my grocery list were cookies and milk, naturally, but I picked up a ton of cold cuts and bread as well. I may have been a wonderful cook, but I had never prepared a hot meal for a huge group of people and I wasn't about to start. Sandwiches were always appreciated, I thought. I had to return to the produce section to get tomatoes and lettuce and cucumbers. I tried not to look over at the oranges.

I went home with my groceries and started cleaning up the house. My father was at the church and had promised I could have the house to myself for the night. He was going to sleep at an associate's place. I was hoping that some of the girls from school would want to sleep over and that the party would turn into a slumber party. Except for Stacy, I had no close friends at school, but then, I hadn't lived in the area long.

Stacy arrived at four to help. She brought two vases of flowers and some Hallowe'en decorations, although Hallowe'en was still a couple weeks away. She festooned the living room with long spiralling orange and black streamers and even carved a pumpkin and put a candle inside it. Stacy thought I had made a mistake not having the party a week later and making it a costume party. But I had purposely chosen to avoid competing with the rash of parties that would begin the following weekend.

At half past seven people began to arrive. I dashed upstairs to change. Actually, I didn't have a lot of clothes to choose from. I settled on a pair of black pants and an orange blouse – in keeping with the season. When I returned downstairs I found that Stacy was letting people in by the carload. I began to relax. I had been afraid that no one would show up. Yet I didn't relax so much that my attention wasn't riveted on the door every time someone new arrived. Where was Christopher? I asked myself. What would Debbie be wearing?

I had a general plan for the night. First, I was going to let people eat and drink and listen to music and mingle. A few people had brought beer, but since I was living in a minister's house I had decided to turn the other cheek – and limit myself to a couple of cans. Then later I was going to have a few organised games, like charades and Trivial Pursuit. I had also bought a tape of old TV theme songs – the object of that game would be to listen to it and identify the programme the particular song had come from. Then I was going to put on a movie, maybe the one I had taped, maybe Stacy's copy of the first *Lethal Weapon*, which she had thoughtfully remembered to bring.

It was close to nine when Christopher came to the front door with Debbie in tow. Debbie was stunning in a short black dress, her blonde hair all over the place, her lips on fire from her bright red lipstick. Christopher had on his usual jeans and T-shirt, but was still the object of all my desires. I greeted them with a wonderfully winning smile and told myself that they seemed happy together. I told them there was food in the kitchen and then ran upstairs to blow my nose and wipe my eyes. But I wasn't devastated. I had been forewarned and life went on. And even though she was cute as pie, I knew Debbie couldn't count the number of brain cells inside her skull on her two hands, even if one of the hands held a pocket calculator.

I next played the tape of old TV show theme songs. Everybody took an index card and a pen and wrote down the name of the show the theme song came from. Naturally, the person who identified the most songs would be the winner. Now, I had never listened to the tape before I put it on, and I hadn't glanced at the card inside the cassette box that listed the TV show. But as I listened to the songs, I knew every one of them – immediately. I hadn't realised I'd watched so much TV growing up. There was *Bewitched* and *Star Trek* and *The Lucy Show* – it was like a nostalgia trip. But I knew I couldn't win my own game at my own party. People would be suspicious. So I set my card aside when people started to read off their choices.

There were thirty songs on the tape. Stacy got twenty-five correct, the highest score. Christopher, even with Debbie's help – I hadn't said *that* wasn't allowed – got only ten right. He said he hadn't watched a lot of TV growing up. But it was Christopher who, just as Stacy was taking her bows, insisted that I reveal how I had done. In fact, he snatched up my card, and his eyes

26

widened when he saw what I had written.

'Hey,' he told everybody. 'Rela got them all right.'

'Did you really?' Stacy asked.

'Well,' I said.

'You cheated,' Stacy said.

'No,' I said.

'Had you listened to the tape before?' Christopher asked.

'No,' I said. 'I just bought it today.' I glared at Stacy. 'I didn't study the paper that came with the cassette, either.'

'How come you didn't tell us you had them all right?' Christopher asked. He was sitting on the couch beside Debbie – who, I had learned, was also new to the area. He was so close his outstretched feet kept bumping into mine. Debbie was staying near him but was not kissing him or anything that would make me want to vomit in her face. I lowered my head at his question.

'I don't like to show off the fact that I spent my formative years in front of the boob tube,' I said.

'She cheated,' Stacy said again. 'I deserve the prize. What is it, Rela?'

I looked over at her. 'You get to keep the tape,' I said.

We went on to charades. Busy with restocking the food, I couldn't play. I was chopping carrot sticks in the kitchen by myself when Christopher walked in. He had a can of beer in his hand, but appeared completely sober. I smiled quickly at him, but it felt strained.

'Looking for the rest room?' I asked.

'No.' He set his beer down on the counter top and settled himself on a stool near me. 'I haven't drunk that much. How are you doing, Rela?'

I kept the smile plastered on my face. 'Oh, I'm just singing in the rain, waiting for it to snow. Are you enjoying the party?'

'It's a great party.'

'You don't like charades?'

He shrugged. 'It's all right, but I wanted a chance to talk to you alone.'

'What?'

'I feel like I never talk to you at school. We're always just passing in the halls.'

I forced a laugh. It's hard for a girl to get near you when you're surrounded by women like Debbie.'

He was puzzled. 'Debbie's my cousin.'

'Really?' I gushed, my bayonet-size vegetable chopping knife in my hand. 'I didn't know that. Wow, that's great – I mean, having such a beautiful cousin.'

He regarded me strangely. 'What made you want to throw a party?'

'I wanted to meet more people at school. I just moved here this summer.'

'Where did you move from?'

I hesitated. I always hated to talk about my past. 'Back east.'

'Are you here with your parents?'

'Yes, my father. I don't have a mother. I'm – It's a long story. How about Debbie? Where's she from?'

'Wisconsin. She just got here last summer.'

'That's when I got here. What a coincidence.'

Christopher grinned. 'You're funny, Rela.'

I chuckled. 'Yeah, I'm hilarious, people die of laughter around me all the time. Hey, I heard that you're applying to Cal Tech.'

He nodded. 'I am, but I'm not sure if I'll get in.'

'You? They'll roll out the red carpet for you. You have a straight A average, don't you? I even heard they've already offered you a scholarship.'

'That's far from definite.'

'What are you going to major in, if you do get in?'

28

'I hope to have a double major in physics and computer science.'

'That's quite a stretch.'

'It might be a lot of work, but I don't see the two subjects as dissimilar. If you think about it much of our subatomic research is already carried out with the help of computers. That will just increase in the future. We have a new generation of computers every ten years. Did you know that scientists at IBM are experimenting with the use of crystals to store data? I just read about it in *Scientific American.* In one stroke we'll be able to access five thousand times quicker.'

'That's amazing,' I said.

'The whole field of computers is exploding. You know how logical processors work now on the serial system? That's where you have all code in binary arrangement – a switch is either on or off. Well, now fuzzy logic is being developed. That's where you have a third choice at the fundamental level of the system. Something is not simply yes or no. It can be maybe.'

I smiled. 'Maybe what?' I wanted to encourage him to talk since he had never really talked to me before for any length of time. Yet I wished he'd change the subject. For all my prowess in mathematics, I had never been comfortable with computers.

'Maybe anything,' Christopher said. 'A thinking machine could be the result of this third choice. It really excites me.' He looked at me shrewdly. 'But it doesn't excite you, does it?'

'I wouldn't say that. I'd say, rather, that it worries me.'

'What? Why? Specifically?'

'I worry that we'll become so dependent on computers that we'll cease to think for ourselves. We'll lose our humanity.'

'You honestly believe that?'

'I do.'

He chuckled. 'You've been watching too many *Terminator* movies. A computer doesn't know anything until it's programmed. Even then it's not conscious.'

'They say it got smart.'

'Pardon?'

'It's my favourite line from the first *Terminator* movie. Maybe it was that line that made me start to worry. I'm a very impressionable young lady.'

Christopher nodded. 'Possibly a machine could become smart, but we'd always know where the off switch was. Anyway, I appreciate your point of view. I'm not the cold young scientist that I appear to be. I'd like to minor in psychology on top of everything else. The human mind fascinates me. Did you know that I have a biofeedback machine in by bedroom? I use it to get into a deep state of alpha. I'd like to show it to you some time.'

Maybe it was the invitation to go to his bedroom that distracted me. Whatever the distraction, I accidentally let my left ring finger stray into the path of the blade as I sliced carrots. The stainless steel cut me almost to the bone before I felt it. A thin film of blood sprayed over my nicely cut carrots. I dropped the knife and raised the wounded finger to my lips. Then I felt the pain. It's amazing how much a bad cut feels like a burn. The coppery taste of blood filled my mouth. Christopher was off his seat and by my side in a second.

'Are you all right?' he asked.

'Ohhh,' I groaned with the finger still in my mouth. This was no tiny nick. The blood was leaking out the sides of my lips and dropping on to my orange blouse. At least, I thought, I would die in his arms.

'Did you cut the finger off?' he asked anxiously. I had spooked him, for sure. He was white.

'I don't know,' I mumbled, lying. 'Check all the carrot sticks to see if one has a ring on it.'

Christopher shook his head, not amused by my humour. He reached out to help me, and I noticed his fingers were shaking. 'I'm taking you to the hospital,' he said.

'No.' I took the finger away from my mouth and the blood dripped on to the cutting board. 'It's my party and I can bleed if I want to.'

'Would you stop joking, Rela? You're really bleeding.'

He was upset, and I felt bad for making him feel worse. For my part, I was calm. The sight of blood didn't really bother me. I grabbed a small dishtowel and wrapped it round the wound. Red blossomed in a circle on the white material. I put pressure on the cut, which wasn't easy to do. The sight of blood might not have bothered me but the pain of the cut did.

'It'll be all right in a few minutes,' I said. 'The bleeding is slowing.'

'Are you sure?' he asked.

'Yes.'

'I still want to take you to the hospital,' Christopher said.

I was touched by his concern, but puzzled at the strength of his reaction. After all, I had cut my finger, not my throat. He continued to breathe rapidly. I smiled to reassure him.

'I'm not going to die, Christopher,' I said gently.

He sat back down on his stool and lowered his head. 'People are so fragile,' he muttered.

I felt such love for him in that moment. It swept over me like a warm wave. Yet – and this was odd – his comment also bothered me. I didn't know why.

'This "people" is not so fragile,' I said, meeting his gaze. He held my eyes a moment before lowering his head as if embarrassed.

'You should get stitches,' he said.

'I'll put a bandage on it. I'll be fine.'

'When did you last get a tetanus shot?'

I laughed. 'I'm not going to get tetanus. Relax!'

Just then Ed of Circuit City fame poked his head in through the door. He had on a tie, and his shirt was straining against his muscles. He looked as if he had just come from work. He made a face when he saw all the blood.

'Having a little argument with your boyfriend, I see,' he said.

'Hi, Ed,' I said. 'No, I just cut my finger. Come in and get something to eat. Just don't sample the carrots. Christopher, this is Ed. He sold me my VCR.'

Ed came in and shook Christopher's hand. 'So you're Rela's guy,' Ed said. 'You don't know how lucky you are to have such a devoted woman. I used every one of my high-powered lines on this girl, and still she wouldn't go out with me. Can you imagine that, turning down Eddie Farmer?'

Christopher took back his hand and put it in his pocket. Ed had obviously enjoyed crushing it. 'That's the trouble with high-powered lines,' Christopher said casually, 'they sometimes give off a lot of static.'

Ed took a step back. 'You sound like Rela.'

'That's because he's not my boyfriend,' I said. 'He's my cousin.'

Christopher glanced at me, amused. Ed was confused. 'Is your boyfriend here?' he asked.

'I don't have one,' I said. 'That was just a line of mine to keep you from hitting on me. But I told Stacy about you and she's more than available.'

Ed brightened. 'Is she that babe who let me in?'

'Probably. Grab some food and go talk to her. We're

going to put on a movie that I recorded with the VCR you sold me.' I groaned involuntarily. The towel I had wrapped round my finger was beginning to throb now. 'This one's going to keep me awake.'

'You should take some aspirin,' Christopher said, still concerned. I decided right then that he could not be present at the birth of our first child. He'd just faint. I had *already* decided I was going to marry him. Despite my physical pain, I was happy that he was showing interest in me.

'I can't,' I said. 'I'm allergic to them. They do funny things to me.'

Ed popped open a can of Coors and grabbed a sandwich. 'Beer does the same thing to my head,' he said and burped.

I went upstairs to take care of my finger. The cut was deep; I was worried it would scar and had second thoughts about Christopher's offer to go to an emergency room. Yet I decided I couldn't leave my party just when it was beginning to roll. I bandaged the finger as best I could and returned to my bedroom. I disconnected the VCR from my TV and carried it downstairs, with the tape inside.

Stacy and Ed met me in the hall off the living room. 'Movie time,' I said.

'Ed tells me you cut off your finger,' Stacy said.

'I was just trying to get Christopher's attention,' I said.

'I thought you said he was your cousin,' Ed said.

'Debbie's Christopher's cousin,' Stacy said.

'You knew that!' I exclaimed.

'No,' Stacy said. 'Debbie just told me.'

'I'm getting confused,' Ed protested.

I brought the VCR into the living room and hollered for attention. I explained what our movie choices were and the majority voted to watch *It!* Handicapped as I was,

I let Christopher hook the VCR up to the TV, which took him about ten seconds. He rewound the tape to the beginning and came over and sat beside me on the couch. Debbie was in the kitchen, or the bathroom maybe – forgotten. My finger pulsed with pain to the pulse of my heart, but I felt content for the first time in a while.

That feeling wasn't to last long.

The movie wasn't at the beginning of the tape, as it should have been. Instead there was news. I wouldn't have been that surprised if it had been the end of a news programme. It was always possible, I thought, especially late at night, that the programme preceding the movie could have run a few minutes over. But clearly the news was just beginning. I jumped up to turn it off.

'I must have programmed in the wrong date,' I said, reaching for the Stop button. I didn't have the remote control on me.

'Wait,' Christopher said. 'You may have just missed the movie. Give it a few minutes.'

'No,' I said. I hit the Stop button on the VCR. The TV screen filled with static. 'I did it wrong.'

'Are you sure?' Ed asked.

'I'm sure,' I said.

'Why don't we fast-forward it a few minutes to check it out,' Stacy suggested, sitting on the floor beside Ed.

'I'm sure, I'm sure,' I snapped, suddenly impatient.

'Rela,' Stacy said.

I took a deep breath. 'We'll watch your movie, Stacy, or else I can run out and rent a couple of movies. OK? Can we just drop it.'

The whole group was staring at me strangely. Christopher stood. 'I wouldn't mind driving over to Blockbuster with you, Rela,' he said.

'We can watch the news until you return,' Ed said.

'That would be too boring,' I said, leaning over and

34

pushing the Eject button. The tape slid into my hand. 'We'll be back in fifteen minutes.'

As Christopher and I were leaving the house, I heard Stacy say, 'I think Rela accidentally recorded a skin flick and knows it.'

The Blockbuster Video outlet was just down the street from my house. My nerves were on edge as I got in Christopher's car for the short hop. He couldn't help but notice my discomfort.

I wouldn't be embarrassed,' he said. 'I often make a mistake programming my VCR. You said yourself it was a new machine.'

I remembered how easily he'd set up the VCR, even with the complexity of the cable box. 'I don't think you make many mistakes.'

'Is your finger bothering you?'

'No, I'm fine, really,' I lied. My hands trembled and I clasped them together in my lap. What was wrong? I wondered. I hadn't wanted to watch *It!* that much. I decided being close to Christopher was intimidating me more than I realised. 'This is a nice car,' I remarked. 'What kind is it?'

'A Mazda 626.'

'Is it yours?'

'Yeah. I just bought it this summer.'

'Nice to have the money,' I said.

'I don't have it now. But I can make it back quick.'

'What do you do?'

He chuckled. 'I fix VCRs, personal computers, stereos, TVs – anything electronic. I used to have to advertise to get business but word of mouth is good now. A few regular technicians in the area bring me their stuff whenever they get backed up.'

'Wow. You've really earned your boy genius nickname.'

'No one calls me that.'

'They do behind your back.'

'Really?'

'Absolutely.'

He smiled. 'You have a nickname, too.'

'I don't believe it. No one at school knows me. What is it?'

'It doesn't matter, but everybody does talk about you.'

'What do they say?'

'I'm not going to tell you.'

'You have to tell me. Is it bad?'

'No,' he said. 'But I'm still not going to tell you.'

'You're driving me crazy.'

'I thought you liked me.'

I blinked. 'What made you think that, Mr Christopher?'

He was taken aback by my serious tone. 'I didn't mean anything by the remark. I just thought, you know, that you didn't find me offensive.'

'That's true. It's true.'

'What's true?'

'It's all true.' I wasn't going to tell him straight to his face that I liked him. I assumed he was pulling my leg when he said people talked about me. There was nothing to talk about, I thought.

I should have realised that that was what people enjoyed gossiping about most.

'How's your finger?' he asked.

'My state of mind is not dictated solely by my sore finger.' I smiled sweetly to let him know I was kidding. 'You don't need to keep asking me that, Christopher.'

He nodded to the video store up ahead. 'We're almost there.'

'Yeah.'

'I've enjoyed talking to you.'

'We should talk some more some time,' he said.

I knew right then he wanted to ask me out. It went straight to my head. 'Yeah. But you know what they say.'

'What do they say?' he asked.

'Talk is cheap.'

He was perceptive. He knew in that moment that I knew of his secret desire for my luscious body. 'Do you want to go out some time?' he asked.

'No.' I was horrible, simply awful.

He seemed disappointed. 'Oh.'

'I'm not allowed to date. My father – he's a minister, you know – has taught me that boys are the straight road to hell.'

He frowned. 'Really? Don't you think that's kind of extreme?'

I shook my head. 'He told me that boys are only interested in one thing. Sex. Sex. Sex. It's only one thing, but he always says it three times, just so I won't forget.'

Chris was offended. 'Not all boys are interested in just sex.'

I acted surprised. 'Really?'

'Yeah.'

I acted disappointed. 'Oh.'

Chris was confused, the poor boy. 'Rela?'

'Yes?'

'Are you pulling my leg?'

I giggled. I can't believe what I said next. The thought of the guy had terrified me the day before and now I was verbally seducing him. 'No, but I'd like to pull on it!' I exclaimed. Then, blushing like a tomato, I clapped my hand over my mouth. Christopher began to laugh softly.

'Where should we go on our first date?' he asked.

I removed my hand. 'Anywhere you want, Mr Christopher.'

FOUR

The bed was not big enough for me and all the things in my dream. I could feel the sheets and blankets constraining me even as I knelt in another room in another place. Christopher was in my dream, too, sitting before a computer screen. I watched from nearby while he pushed a button and a fantastically complex map of the interior of a human brain flowed out. Together we journeyed along the pathways of the neurons, the synapses firing like miniature bolts of lightning in caves that had never seen the light of day – caves of consciousness that could nevertheless imagine the sun of a galaxy a million light-years away. Christopher spoke softly, clearly, yet I couldn't understand everything he said. The brain on the screen pulsed with blood, even as my own heart beat rapidly. The rhythm of the beat filled the room. Christopher was showing me the secrets of the universe. He had found them in the most surprising place of all. Inside human kind – in the depths of souls.

But somewhere in the journey I felt I had lost my soul. The room with Christopher and the computer slowly faded and was replaced by a bedroom, sparsely furnished. I sat there on the edge of a chair before a small table on which lay a vial of green liquid and a brand-new syringe. The green solution sparkled as I held it up to the light and stared into its depths. But not with life. It sparkled as a crystal in a computer circuit would. I knew somehow the solution had something to do with memory, but I didn't know if it stored it or wiped it clean. I stabbed the needle into the vial and drew out the solution. Then I slid the needle into a vein in my arm. As the green fluid poured into my blood, I felt it penetrate my heart, my soul, until all I knew of humanity was lost. Everything became grey, grey as a winter sky that promised only bitter cold and frost.

Then came a long interval when I floated, when I was carried through the air on impersonal currents of wind or perhaps the even more indifferent arms of machines. I couldn't say which because I couldn't say what I was. Finally I settled down and cold liquid swelled around me, over my legs and hips, across my chest and arms, until it reached my face. Even here the liquid did not stop. It covered my face, smothering me and taking away my breath. I drank in the cold, became the cold. Time stopped, and everything was black, black as death without meaning . . .

I woke up stark naked in my bathtub. The water was turned on, and was running cold and hard. It was bubbling over my lower lip. Another few seconds unconscious and I would have drowned. I coughed and sat suddenly upright. The bathroom was dark but I could see the gooseflesh on my arms and legs.

'Rela,' I whispered to myself. 'You had way too much to drink.'

Yet that wasn't true. I only drank two cans of beer. Two cans shouldn't have sent me sleepwalking to the bathtub. I clearly remembered climbing into bed with my pyjamas on.

I didn't remember my dream clearly, not at first. Only the green fluid and the long silver needle I had shoved into my vein. I shivered and climbed out of the tub. I noticed the light in my bedroom was on. Odd, I thought.

A few minutes later I was downstairs in the living room, dry with my blue polka-dot pyjamas on. I had gone downstairs to make myself a glass of warm milk but settled on to the sofa in front of the TV instead. I had yet to put on a light, but could see the tape resting on top of the VCR clearly enough. The tape that was supposed to have *It!* on it, the horror movie of my childhood, the source of so many of my nightmares. More of my dream came back to me then. I remembered Christopher staring deep into the human brain, the feeling I'd had watching him, that he could take me there with him. That I, too, could know the secrets of the universe.

'Weird,' I muttered. Where did my subconscious get such ideas?'

I tried to push the dream aside, but I didn't get up and go into the kitchen. I continued to sit and stare at the tape. For the life of me, I couldn't understand how I had made a mistake programming the machine. The instructions had been simple enough and I wasn't a fool. The only thing I could think of was that I had started with the wrong date. Perhaps there had been a news programme on twenty-four hours earlier, and I had set it to record that instead of the movie. Checking such a hypothesis would be easy. I'd just have to look in the *TV Guide.* Yet I didn't feel inclined to do so. I just kept staring at the tape in the dark, wondering why it scared me so.

'It's just the news,' I said out loud. 'The news is not scary. It's always happening far away and to someone else.'

But this time I felt like something was happening to me. I was cold still from my unplanned bath, and keenly alert. In fact, it had to be three or four in the morning and I didn't feel the least bit drowsy. My fear might have been keeping me awake, but I felt there was something else helping. I was excited,

40

I realised. I was excited about the tape.

But why?

Slowly I rose from the couch and picked the tape up off the VCR. I had put it there after the last person to leave the party – Stacy – was safely out the door. Previous to that I had quietly sat in the living room with my friends watching *Them!* – an old sci-fi movie about gigantic killer antlike creatures. Christopher had been the next to the last person to leave and had promised to call tomorrow. Life was good. Why was I getting so excited about a news tape then?

'Why not play it and quit talking to yourself?' I said out loud.

I slid the tape into the VCR; the machine practically snatched it out of my hand. After turning on the TV, I slowly backed away to sit on the couch. Just before the middle-aged male announcer came on the screen I remembered more of my dream, the holographic map of the human brain. I wondered whose brain Christopher had chosen to map.

'Good morning, people,' the announcer began. 'Our top story today. In the Middle East, peace talks between the Arab and Jewish community . . .'

The news droned on. There was nothing special about it: fighting in Iraq; space shuttle unable to get a new satellite out of its cargo bay; more people out of work. I began to relax, to feel silly. I'd just thrown a wonderful party, had the guy of my dreams ask me out – now it was the middle of the night, and I was sitting on my couch watching a day-old news programme. I should have been sleeping, dreaming of what was to happen next in my love life.

Only how old was this news programme?

The announcer had moved on to sport. It was football season.

'The Raiders looking good,' the man was saying. 'Twenty-one to seventeen over the Steelers. Down in Miami the Dolphins suffered a real setback, losing to the last-place Patriots, zero to three. Up in Minnesota the Vikings were incredible, crushing the Redskins forty-six to seven . . .'

As I was saying, it was football season. Naturally the guy should have been talking about the games that day. Yet I was suddenly overwhelmed with an uneasy feeling. It took me a minute to pinpoint why. It was early Sunday morning. I knew football was played on both Saturday and Sunday. But college ball was usually played on Saturday; the pros played on Sunday.

Yet this announcer was giving out the scores for professional teams.

As if it were early *Monday* morning.

I chuckled. 'So what?' I said out loud to myself. I was fond of talking to myself. 'The scores are from last Sunday.'

Yeah, right, I thought, a tenth of a second later. The news announcer had nothing better to do than report last week's football scores, and talk about the games as if they had just happened a few hours earlier.

It was time I checked the *TV Guide.* I didn't have to turn on the light as I flipped through it. The glow from the tube was sufficient to read by. In a moment I found the page for Saturday. *It!* was listed for October 15, Saturday, 3:00 A.M. I traced the time slot back day by day, but didn't come to a news programme in the time period until October 10. There would be a news programme on at three in the morning two days *after It!* was supposed to have been shown, on October 17. Indeed, there was a news show on *every* Monday at that hour. I set the programme guide aside and searched for the paper we'd received Saturday morning. The date on

42

it said October 15. That made sense to me. That was the date I had programmed in when I had set the machine to record *It!* I knew for a fact I had put in the correct date because I had put it in with the movie schedule sitting on my lap. The date at present, because it was already Sunday, was October 16.

But, I remembered, I had not set the initial date when I'd had the movie schedule. I had done that earlier, right after taking the machine out of the box and plugging it in. Then I had run up and down between my bedroom and the kitchen, while I cooked dinner for my father and completed the programming. Was it possible my initial date had been off by a few days?

Easy to settle that. I squinted at the date in blue block characters on the upper right-hand corner of the VCR.

It read October 18.

'There,' I said aloud. 'That was my mistake. I was off by two days when I set the date. No worries. Now I can go to bed and dream of Christopher taking me to Paris in the jet he's built in his spare time.'

Oh, but hold on, little girl. Wait just one minute. Maybe wait a couple of days. I may have made a mistake, I realised, but so had the logical progression of the universe. I still shouldn't have been able to record the news two days in advance.

So, what had happened?

I had set the machine to record exactly two days after the time slot when *It!* was supposed to be on. By chance, news was on then. By chance I had recorded the news.

Two days before the news was supposed to be on.

'Impossible,' I whispered.

It hit me then and it hit me hard.

I had recorded Monday morning's news.

I had taped the future.

FIVE

Late Sunday afternoon I sat with my father and watched the Raiders play the Steelers. I was waiting for Christopher to come over to take me to dinner, and I wanted to see if I'd got a better deal on my VCR than I thought.

Christopher had called me around noon to *tell* me where we were going. It was a restaurant down by the beach. Sounded romantic to me. He was supposed to pick me up at five, but after he called all the clocks in the house seemed to be broken because it took for ever for the evening to come.

I hadn't planned on watching the Raiders-Steelers game, but my father had it on and I had time to kill, so I ended up watching it from the beginning of the fourth quarter. The score at that point was fourteen to zero in favour of the Steelers. I remembered the Raiders were supposed to win twenty-one to seventeen. My confidence in the prescient ability of my VCR was still high. The fact that the Raiders and the Steelers were playing each other at all was already powerful confirmation I had recorded a future event.

'The Raiders will score three touchdowns in the final quarter and win the game twenty-one to seventeen,' I said to my father. He had been happy that the party had gone well, and I was feeling guilty for asking him not to come home since no one had ended up staying over. My father looked particularly tired, and I hoped his heart wasn't acting up. He shook his silver-covered head at my suggestion.

'The way they're playing today they'll be lucky to get in the end zone once,' he said.

'Do you want to bet on it?' I asked.

My father was interested. Although he was a Methodist minister, he loved Las Vegas, gambling of all kinds, particularly blackjack. He was pretty liberal when it came to the rules of the Lord. In fact, he once told me that he believed God had thrown the dice when he created the world.

'How much?' he asked.

'A hundred bucks.'

'You said you spent all your money on your VCR. How are you going to pay me if you lose?'

'I'm not going to lose.'

'I want an I.O.U.'

I smiled. 'Fine. But if I win I want the cash.'

'What kind of odds do you want?'

'What do you mean?'

'You are giving me an exact score, Rela. You deserve better than an even payment if you're correct. I'll give you ten-to-one odds.'

'Five-to-one.'

'Ten-to-one is better for you. If I lose I have to pay you a thousand dollars.

'Five-to-one. I don't want to take all your money.'

I shook with anticipation. 'Let's see, what can I buy with five hundred dollars?'

'Don't count your chickens before they hatch,' my father warned. He gestured to the TV. 'The Steelers are deep in Raider territory again. They'll probably score.'

'A field goal, maybe. It'll be the last time they score.'

The Steelers scored two minutes later – a field goal. The Raiders got the ball. There were twelve minutes left in the game. They brought in a new quarterback, some young guy just out of college. Talented but green, the announcer said. The new quarterback didn't know that. He marched the Raiders down the field for a touchdown in four minutes, the last play being a tightly thrown spiral to a receiver in the corner of the end zone. Score: Steelers seventeen, Raiders seven.

'They have to score twice more for you to win,' my father said. 'They don't have time.'

'I think I'll get a new dress. No, two new dresses.'

'When's your young man supposed to be here?' he asked.

'Sixteen minutes and thirty-two seconds.'

My father smiled. 'You really like this guy.'

'You'll love him. He's the smartest guy in the school. He's cute, too. A real hunk.'

My father laughed. 'Sounds like love.' Then his face fell as he looked at the TV. 'The Steelers just fumbled the ball on the kickoff. The Raiders recovered it on the Steelers' ten-yard line.'

I rubbed my hands together in anticipation. 'Another touchdown coming up. I think I need a new coat for winter.'

'Do you have a coat?' my father asked seriously.

I stared at the TV. 'I don't think so.'

'I'll buy you one.'

I smiled faintly. 'I'll be able to get my own soon.'

'Rela?'

'Yes.'

'How are you doing?'

'Good.'

'Everything's all right at school?'

'Yes. I'm getting all As.'

46

'You know I'm very proud of you.'

'I know. I'm very proud of you, too. All the work you do for the homeless. I wish I had time to help you out.'

'Why don't you come down to the mission some time?'

'It's hard,' I said. 'With school and my job at the library.'

Out of the corner of my eye I could see my father watching me. 'Is there anything you want to talk about, Rela?' he asked.

'No.'

'If ever you want to talk, I'm always here.'

'I know.'

The Raiders scored a touchdown a couple of minutes after recovering the fumble. The Steelers got the ball back but couldn't do anything with it. They had to kick off to the Raiders with five minutes left. The score was Raiders fourteen, Steelers seventeen. Once more the Raiders began to march up the field, taking their time, using up the clock so their next score would be the last one. My father began to grow uncomfortable.

'I can't believe this is happening,' he said.

'I should have a better stereo,' I said. 'New CDs.'

Christopher arrived when the Raiders were on the Steelers' four-yard line and there were twelve seconds left. I ran to the door, opened it, grabbed him by the arm, and dragged him into the living room to see the climatic play. My father was to be forgiven for hardly glancing at Christopher.

'Here it goes,' my father muttered.

'All five hundred of it,' I agreed.

'Who's playing?' Christopher asked.

'Shh,' we both said.

The ball was hiked. The young green quarterback –
who was looking more and more like Joe Montana –
faked a handoff to his running back and rolled to the
right. He had a man open in the corner of the end
zone again. Zip! The pass was high but the receiver
could jump. Touchdown. Time expired. The game was
over.

Twenty-one to seventeen. Exactly.

'Yes!' I shouted, jumping off my seat. 'Five hundred
bucks!'

My father buried his head in his hands. 'I have a bona
fide psychic living in my house.'

'Cash,' I said to my father, slapping him on the back.
'I want cash.'

'Did you two gamble on the game or what?'
Christopher asked.

'It wasn't a gamble,' I said. 'It was a sure thing.'

My father stared up at me with a strange expression
on his face. He didn't care about the money, I knew.
I wasn't even going to take it from him if he did offer
to give it to me. It was all in fun. At least that's what I
thought. Yet there was fear on my father's face.

'How did you know the score?' my father asked.

I stopped bouncing around and shrugged. 'It was just
a guess.'

He continued to watch me. 'It was a hell of a guess,'
he said.

Christopher drove us to the oceanside restaurant, which
was exquisite and situated on a hill directly above the
crashing waves. Christopher had made reservations and
we were led to a table by the window. A candle flame
shimmered between us. The sun had recently set over
the watery horizon. I pleased Christopher by telling him
he could order for me.

'I don't care what I eat as long as it's expensive,' I said.

'Then you should have lobster,' he said with a smile. For the first time I noticed how curious his smile was. Even though he was young, his smile seemed somehow ancient and sad. I told him what I thought.

'I have the weight of the world on me,' he joked.

'You mean that.'

He shrugged. 'No.'

I nodded. 'You feel as if you're destined for great things.'

'I just feel hungry, Rela.'

'I had a dream about you,' I said suddenly.

He was interested – I could tell because he gave me his cue: he always raised his left eyebrow when his interest was piqued, like Mr Spock on *Star Trek*. 'Oh? Tell me about it.'

'We were sitting together in what looked like your study. You were older. You had a computer beside you and you were showing me an internal map of a brain . . .' My voice faltered.

'Go on,' he said.

I turned my head to the right, in the direction of the ocean. The window beside us was open and I could feel the gentle tug of the salty breeze on my bare arms. I don't know why I suddenly turned to peer out into the darkening blue. A wave of cold swept over me and I drew in a breath, which only made me tremble. I swallowed heavily.

'I can't remember any more,' I said, lying.

'Rela?'

I forced a smile. 'Yes?'

'Are you all right?'

'Yes. Actually, I wanted to tell you about that VCR I bought. It's amazing. It—' Again my voice faltered.

Christopher waited for me to continue. I forced another smile. I wanted to tell him about what had happened; I'd been dying to, but all at once I didn't want to. I just felt that it would be—

A mistake. A dangerous mistake.

Yes, I sensed danger. But I wasn't sure if I sensed it emanating from him or from myself.

'It makes incredible tapes,' I said finally.

He visibly relaxed. 'Did *It!* show up later on the tape?'

'No.'

'There was just the news?'

My voice sounded false. 'That's all there was.'

The waitress came and Christopher ordered and we spoke about other things: school, college, music. I was surprised to learn he could play the piano. I was fairly accomplished on the instrument myself. My father would sometimes ask me to play him some Bach before he went to bed at night. He said it soothed his nerves. Christopher was impressed that I could read music.

'Where did you learn?' he asked.

'My grandfather taught me,' I said. 'My real one.'

'As opposed to the fake one?'

I hesitated. 'I'm adopted.'

The revelation shocked him, as it had Stacy. 'So you know who your real parents are,' he said.

'No.'

'But you know your grandfather?' he asked.

'Well, it's a long story.'

'You don't have to talk about it if you don't want to.'

'It's in the past, and it's boring.' The waitress was bringing our food. 'I'd rather eat.'

So we ate our dinner and I discovered a few small things about Christopher that reassured me that I could live happily ever after with him. He had good manners – he didn't chew with his mouth open or talk while he was chewing. Also he wasn't in love with himself. He had confidence, extraordinary faith in his abilities for someone still in high school, but he quietly accepted his intelligence as a gift rather than as something to set him above other kids. He also seemed to be interested in me, a quality I prized in him above all others.

Since it was Sunday night and we both had school and work the next day, Christopher took me straight home from the restaurant. I was disappointed at his sensible approach. I invited him in as we pulled into the driveway. He declined.

'I have to fix a couple of VCRs before I go to bed,' he said.

'I think I'll try programming mine to tape something in the middle of the night,' I said. The middle of *tomorrow* night, I thought.

He reached out and touched my left shoulder. He hadn't touched me all night, not even my hand. 'I had fun tonight,' he said.

I smiled. 'It was magic.'

He laughed. 'I never know when you're kidding.'

I touched his hand. 'I'm not always, you know. I had a good time, too.'

'We should get together again.'

'I work Monday, Wednesday, and Friday, but otherwise I'm around.'

'Maybe we could do something next weekend,' he suggested.

'Yeah.' Next weekend sounded like a thousand years away. Little did I know I would feel like I had aged a thousand years by the time Wednesday arrived. 'Or this Tuesday night would be good.'

He squeezed my shoulder, his smile broadening. 'I'll try to get free for Tuesday. What would you like to do?'

'See a movie – two movies.'

'How do you like your popcorn?'

'Dry, plain – without butter.' I paused. 'How do you like your girls?'

'The same.'

I sneered. 'Plain like me, right?'

He kissed me then, suddenly, quickly. It was little more than a peck, but it made my entire life worthwhile. 'I like a little salt,' he said as he drew back. He looked so cute, kind of like a Christmas package that I wanted to tear the wrappings off to see what was inside. But I knew that would have to wait.

'Good night, Mr Christopher,' I said, opening my car door.

'Good night, Girl Genius.' He saw my confusion.

'*That's* your nickname at school.' He shrugged. 'You and I have the same one. I don't know if that means anything.'

SIX

Another nightmare. Another horror. But I saw more than I felt. Had I felt everything my mind would have split in two. Yet I suffered enough, God, yes.

They took me out of the freezing bath. *They* – faceless shadows with strong arms. They carried me to the orange room filled with the cold steam. The reclining chair with the white sheets waited for me. But the sheets were not brand-new as I had believed at first; they were already stained with drops of blood. The faceless figures set me down carefully. I felt the slight bump, yet I couldn't feel my skin. It seemed that I had only empty space to cover me.

The chair was highly mechanised. Braces rose and then lowered to clamp down on my head and waist and ankles, immobilising me. Motors whirled and the chair elongated into a bed as it slowly revolved in space. Finally I was strapped and held in an upright position before a wide blank computer screen. Then a large section of the back of the chair – or the bed – was removed and I could feel icy fingers probe my spine. It was then I realised I was being made ready for an operation.

Yet they gave me no anaesthetic.

They were just going to start cutting.

I heard a high whining, like that of a dentist's drill.

The shadows at the edge of my vision moved closer.

The sound went into my back. No pain.

But blood began to drop on to the smooth white floor below me.

My blood. I screamed but made no sound.

The computer screen came on.

It showed an internal map of the spinal cord, millions of microscopic nerve fibres twisted together to form one living rope. Yet the cord looked dark. The miniature saw whined as it cut through the length of my back, and I could feel metal rods being inserted along it. Then there came a horrendous yank, followed by a moist tearing sound.

They had torn my spine from my body.

My screams blazed in my frozen soul like flames through a crystal cave. But the cave remained cold and the shadows moved around in front of me. The computer screen switched to the map of my brain. Yes, it was my brain they had mapped, not Christopher's. I thought of him then, and I cursed him. Why hadn't he been able to spare me this agony?

A steel blade glistened in the orange light before me.

A gloved hand pressed it on to the top of my skull.

This I could feel – the metal teeth fastening into my skin.

They began to saw. The noise. The blood.

The sorrow of it all.

Yet my eyes – they must have left those intact. I watched as the eye of the computer screen took me deeper into my brain, even as the indifferent fingers probed the underlying layers of my grey tissue. Here, it was also dark. No synapses with shooting molecular bolts of lightning. Not a single neuron glowed with the memory of days spent beneath the sun. The pathways of consciousness were as silent as my pleas for help. There was life, yet not life as I knew it.

Not life as God had created it at the beginning of time.

I saw a flash of silver. It was horrible. It was the seed of the curse – that I knew for a fact, even if the shadows did not. Yet it was also brilliant. The seed could reveal the secrets of the universe.

It was my destiny to know them all.

'Jesus,' I whispered as I sat upright in bed.

My room was bright – the light was on. Had I forgotten to turn it off before sleeping? I never did that. I was in bed, dry, not sitting in the bathtub. I could hear my heart pounding, my laboured breathing. Down the hall, my father snored peacefully. The house was otherwise silent. Before me, on the far side of the room, sat the dark screen of my TV. On top of it rested my VCR. I had set it to record the late news for the following day. I couldn't tell if the machine had done anything yet.

I picked up the remote control beside my bed and pushed the Rewind button. I didn't expect anything to happen. I had put a new tape into the machine before going to bed and if nothing had been recorded, the tape should have been at the beginning.

Yet the tape began to rewind inside the machine.

I remembered every detail from my dream.

I trembled on my bed. A minute passed.

The tape stopped rewinding.

A different announcer. A woman. Pretty. Great hair.

'Good evening,' she said. 'In the news tonight: Saudi Arabia is protesting the recent loan guarantees to Israel saying the Israelis have not contributed substantially to the peace negotiations going on in—'

I listened for fifteen minutes before I learned that I had recorded the news over twenty hours before it was to be broadcast.

'It taped while I slept,' I said aloud. Just like before.

The baseball play-offs were on. The Oakland As were playing the Toronto Blue Jays on Monday night.

I wrote it down and went back to sleep.

No more dreams. For now.

SEVEN

I didn't go to school on Monday. I drove to Las Vegas instead. It took me four hours. I wanted to bet on the As-Blue Jays game and I knew such gambling was illegal in Los Angeles. Since I didn't have a bookie, Vegas was my only choice. Before I left I asked my father for the five hundred bucks. He was surprised by my request, although he said he'd had every intention of honouring his bet. I promised I'd give him the money back that evening. We had to drive to the bank to get the cash. I figured I'd need cash in Vegas. My father was a gem – he didn't even ask me what I needed the money for. He told me to keep it, that I had won it fair and square.

The drive across the desert passed uneventfully. I had never been to Las Vegas before, and I must say I loved everything about it. The size of some of the hotels blew me away. I had heard good things about the Mirage so I went there first. The casino was fairly empty when I entered; it was two o'clock in the afternoon. I asked a woman refilling a slot machine where I could bet on the game and she directed me to an area where there were numerous giant-screen TVs with rows of empty seats set before them, sort of like a miniature theatre, or better yet, arena. A number of horse races were presently being televised on the screens. There was a counter on the right side, boxed in with metal bars.

A grisly old man in a hotel uniform looked at me as I stepped up to the counter.

'Looking for your parents?' he asked.

I had on a black dress and had put my hair up to make me look older. I knew you had to be twenty-one to gamble in Vegas. I also knew the rule was seldom strictly enforced.

'My daughter,' I said smoothly and smiled. The man appraised me closely and I returned the favour. He had so many lines on his face he could have lain out in the sun with the cacti on his lunch breaks. He wasn't frail, though. The muscles under the skin on his bare arms were firm. His hair was dark. I could tell he dyed it, but still he had plenty of it. He pulled an unlit cigar from the corner of his mouth and nodded at my purse.

'Are you here to place a bet?' he asked.

'Yes.'

'How old are you, young lady?'

'Twenty-one.'

He scowled. 'My ass.'

I beamed. 'Your ass is twenty-one, too? What month was it born?'

He sighed. 'Oh, brother. Do you have any I.D.?'

'How often do you ask for I.D.?'

'Never. But you've already pissed me off. Where's your driver's licence?'

'I don't have one. But I have five hundred dollars in cash. I want to bet on tonight's baseball game.'

He looked more interested. 'Do you like baseball?'

'I love it. I'm a big fan of the As.'

'God was in a good mood the day he invented baseball,' the man said. 'Are you here with your parents?'

'Nope. I'm sorry to say that they've both already died of old age.' I put my arms on the counter top and leaned in closer towards him. 'I'm filthy rich,' I said confidentially. 'You don't have to worry about me losing my money.'

He snorted. 'I'm worried about losing my job. You have to be twenty-one to place a bet here.'

'I am twenty-one.' I withdrew the five one-hundred-dollar bills from my purse, letting him see them. 'You have my word of honour.'

'You want to put that all on the As?'

'Nope. I'm betting against them. They're going to lose tonight nine to one. I want to wager that as the exact score and I want odds.'

'I can tell you what the odds on that would be right now.' He turned to a blackboard behind him that was lettered with columns and rows of numbers. 'Forty-eight to one.'

I did a little mental arithmetic. 'Are you saying if I bet this five hundred dollars and win, you will pay me twenty-four thousand dollars?'

'No. Those are the straight odds. We will automatically take ten per cent off that amount. If you wager five hundred dollars that the Blue Jays will win nine to one over the As, and if you're right, we'll pay you twenty-one thousand six hundred.'

I pushed the money forward. 'I'll take it.'

He pushed the money back. 'That's a fool's bet.'

'I told you, I'm a rich fool.'

He put his cigar back in his mouth. 'What's your name?'

'Rela.'

'I'm Bob.' He offered me a hairy hand through the bars.

'Pleased to meet you, Bob. I told you not to worry about me or your job. If I lose, I lose. I won't make any fuss. If I win, it's pennies to me.'

'How did you come up with that score, Rela?'

'I'm psychic.'

He leaned forward. If he hadn't been so old I would have thought he was the Marlboro Man himself; the smell of tobacco on his breath was incredible.

'I've been in this business a long time,' he said. 'I've met a lot of psychics. They usually end up at Gamblers Anonymous – flat broke. You're going to lose that five hundred dollars as sure as a snake spits in the desert. And you're not rich, Rela. I can tell by looking at you.'

I was insulted. 'How can you tell?'

'Your shoes. It's always the shoes. Where did you get them? K-mart?'

'JC Penneys – on sale. Look, Bob, accept my bet. If I win I'll buy you dinner. We can get drunk together.'

'Are you old enough to drink?'

I held his eye. 'I have an inside tip on this game. I can't explain it to you. You just have to believe me. Take my bet and make a bet of your own.'

He may have been impressed with my earnestness. He sighed again and stared at my money. 'You sure this won't break you?' he asked.

'I've got it covered. Bet with me. It'll be the best bet you ever made.'

'I'd have to go to another casino to place a bet on the game. I can't do it here.' For the first time he regarded me seriously. 'How good is your tip?'

'Good as gold. Nine to one will be the score.'

'You can't predict that. No one can.'

'I'm telling you the truth. Do I look crazy?'

'You sound crazy, Rela.' But then he relaxed and shrugged his shoulders. 'Maybe I'll put twenty on it, just to please you.'

'Put a hundred on it,' I said firmly.

He shook his head. 'This town attracts all kinds.'

*

Later, when the sun had set and the Strip was ablaze with lights, I returned to the Mirage to collect my winnings. I figured Bob would be off work but I found him waiting in one of the chairs arranged in front of the giant TV screens. He jumped up when he saw me.

'I don't know why I did it,' he said, 'but I put my whole paycheque on your hunch.'

I was delighted. 'How much did you make?'

He was excited. 'Almost as much as you did. Here to collect your money? You got that slip I made out for you?'

'Yeah, I didn't lose it.' I fished it out of my pocket and handed it to him. He moved towards the counter.

'I'm not on the job right now but I'll see to it that you get your money promptly,' he said. He called for a young man in the back and handed him the slip and whispered something in his ear. Bob turned to me. 'I assume you want cash?'

'Yes.'

'Will hundreds be OK?'

'Perfect.'

He gestured to the other guy, who disappeared into the back. Bob stepped close and put his arm around me. He had brushed his teeth or gargled since we talked earlier. His breath was mint fresh. He had on nice clothes, too.

'How did you do it?' he asked.

'Can't tell you.'

'Come on.'

'Nope. That's your one tip. You can torture me and you won't get it out of me.'

He laughed. 'I knew you were going to say that. Did you know I quit my job? I'm leaving town tonight. Flying back to New York for a long holiday. That's home. Mind if we have that dinner another time?'

'That's fine. I have to drive back to L.A. But you have to tell me, why did you listen to me? I never thought you'd risk so much.'

My question puzzled him. He took his arm from my shoulder and stepped back and got a funny look in his eye. He was happy but he was afraid.

'There's just something about you, Rela' was all he would say.

EIGHT

I didn't get back to L.A. until one in the morning. Just for the hell of it I drove by Christopher's house. I knew where he lived. It was a one-storey house with a light on in one room. I guessed it was his. Summoning my courage – winning a lot of money had given me a shot of adrenaline and nerve – I parked and walked up to his open window and knocked lightly. Almost immediately he pulled aside the curtain. He had electrodes taped to his head and a weird smile on his face that made me take a step back.

'Hi,' he said as if I stopped by every night.

'Are you on this planet?' I asked.

'Barely. Should I let you in?'

'Will we wake up your parents?' I asked.

A minute later he let me in the front door. He had taken off his electrodes. The second I was in his bedroom he closed the door and pointed to his biofeedback machine. A foot-square black box, it sat on the far right of his cluttered wooden desk. It had a row of three control knobs and four sets of wires leading away from it. Above each knob were different coloured lights. Christopher explained that each light corresponded to a different brain wave: theta, alpha, beta, delta. He said the combination of alpha and theta was the best.

'When your brain produces those waves you get in a really high state,' he said enthusiastically.

'What's it feel like?' I asked, taking a seat on the corner of his bed. His room was jammed with scientific paraphernalia: a telescope, a microscope, two computers, maps of the nighttime sky. A perfect room for a young Einstein. He sat in his desk chair and put his bare feet up on the bed beside me. He had on grey tracksuit bottoms, no shirt. The muscles of his chest were well defined, his skin hairless. I wanted to rub his feet but it was late and I wasn't so bold.

'You feel euphoric,' he said. 'It's as if you're melting into and becoming part of a vast ocean.'

'Is it like how the yogis describe higher states of consciousness?'

He brushed his hand aside. 'They describe their experiences in mystical terms. There is nothing mystical about this. When the brain produces certain waves your consciousness is naturally altered.'

'Could it be the other way round?'

'What do you mean?' he asked.

'Could the fact that your consciousness alters change your brain waves?'

'No.' He tapped his biofeedback machine. 'With this I can control my brain waves directly. It's purely a mechanical process.'

I smiled. 'But you're not a machine, Christopher.'

He nodded, also smiling. 'You're getting into heavy philosophical territory. Are our minds the result of our brains or is it the other way around? I, for one, see no evidence that our consciousness is anything more than the result of electrochemical activity inside our brains.'

'You don't believe that we have souls?' I asked.

'No. I think that's only a fool's wish. Are you religious?'

'My father's a minister.'

'You didn't answer the question.'

I closed my eyes a moment. The terror of my recent nightmares touched me briefly then. Yet something in these dreams, horrible as they were, made me feel that, yes, there was a part of me that could survive any catastrophe. I opened my eyes.

'It depends on what you mean by religious,' I said. 'I believe in life.'

'That's vague. What do you believe about life?'

'That it's beautiful. That it goes on and on.'

'That's one thing life certainly doesn't do. The redwoods may live two thousand years, but in the end they die. Unless there's an amazing medical breakthrough soon, we'll both be dead eighty years from now.'

'I suppose,' I said wistfully. The conversation was depressing me. I wondered how it had got started. I had stopped by to show Christopher my stack of hundred dollar bills, but now I hesitated. He'd want to know how I'd got the money and my reluctance to discuss my VCR was still strong. It was nice, though, just to sit on his bed and be with him. I added, 'What are you doing up so late?'

'I could ask you the same question,' he said. 'I often stay up late to work.'

'Fixing VCRs and stuff?'

'No. I do that during the day. At night I work on my own stuff.'

'Such as?'

He chuckled. 'I'm building a starship. Would you like to be my chief engineer?'

'Sounds like fun.'

He stood and reached for the electrodes he had been wearing. 'I want to hook you up to my biofeedback machine.'

'Does it hurt?'

'Not at all.' He gestured for me to sit in his chair. 'The wires won't reach to the bed.'

I moved into the chair reluctantly. 'Could I accidentally get electrocuted?'

He laughed as he began to probe my head searching for a good place to attach the wires, brushing aside my hair where it was in his way. A week ago I would have believed his touching my head would be a heavenly experience. Now I was trembling with fear.

'You'll live, Rela,' he said.

'I don't know if I like this.'

'You'll love it. You can do it with your eyes open or closed. A different light goes on every time your brain produces a particular wave. The machine allows you to train your brain consciously to make alpha or theta – whatever. But the machine also makes a specific sound for the different waves you make. Once you know the sound you don't have to watch the lights any more. You can lie back and go deep.'

'Deep,' I whispered.

'Yes,' he promised. He pulled back the hair on my right temple, and I could feel the wire lightly scratch my skin. Impossible as it may sound, I could smell the copper in the wire, and it reminded me of another smell, that of blood, which also contained copper. My nightmares were never really that far from my consciousness. It was odd, I thought, how they had started when I bought the VCR. Christopher continued, 'Here, let me just stick this contact beside your—'

'Stop,' I said, standing up suddenly and pulling the electrodes off.'

He seemed surprised. 'What's wrong?'

I was having trouble breathing. 'I don't know.'

'Rela.'

'I don't want to do it.'

'I swear to you there is absolutely no danger. These wires only receive the very low voltage your brain is producing. They don't carry any electricity into the brain.'

A wave of dizziness came over me, and the room swam before my eyes. I stepped towards the door. 'I have to go home. I'm sorry.'

'Rela.' He grabbed my arm. 'You don't have to do it.' He put his other hand on my shoulder and pulled me closer. 'You don't have to go. Look at you, you're trembling.'

I lowered my head, embarrassed. The dizziness was passing as swiftly as it had come. 'I guess my brain must be producing Rela waves,' I said softly.

He gently lifted my chin. 'What are Rela waves?' he asked.

'They're incoherent. They make people believe in butterflies and trees.'

Christopher watched me with his deep, dark eyes, but I did not see the moon and the stars in them this time. I saw only a young man who liked dangerous toys, and it didn't matter to me that he said they were safe. Yet for all that it didn't make me love him any less. He touched my hair.

'Those are not such bad things.' he said.

'I like them.'

'Did I ever tell you that you looked familiar to me when we met?'

I was surprised. 'You looked familiar to me, too.'

'Really?'

'Yeah. Right from the beginning. Why do you think that is?'

'I don't know. I don't know if it matters.'

'It matters to me.'

'You look sad. Are you sad?'

I frowned. 'Yes,' I said honestly.

'Too many Rela waves.' He leaned closer. 'Can I kiss you?'

I smiled. 'You're not supposed to ask. You're just supposed to do it.' I paused. 'No.'

He grinned. 'Is this no the same no you gave me when I asked you out?'

'No.' I stepped back and his hand fell away from my hair. 'I can't tonight, Christopher. It's not a good time for me.'

He was concerned. 'You're still upset. I'm sorry I scared you.'

'You didn't scare me. I scared myself.' I turned towards the door. 'I've got to get home before it's too late.'

'Too late for what?'

I paused at the door and glanced over my shoulder. Déjà vu touched me. There was no denying it. I had seen Christopher before in his bedroom – a long time ago. Yet not in *this* room.

'Too late for the news,' I said. 'I want to watch it.'

NINE

But I didn't watch the news that night. I slept instead, and I had dreams, many, but I couldn't remember them as well as the others, and for that I was thankful.

I waited until the morning to turn on my TV and VCR. Early Tuesday morning I watched the news for Tuesday night in my bedroom. The announcer was new – an exotic redheaded female. My machine's magic worked on any channel. I had programmed it right after leaving Christopher's house, just before going to sleep.

The news was gruesome.

'This afternoon at approximately twelve o'clock at the Hyatt Hotel in downtown San Francisco tragedy struck,' the announcer said. 'A team of four window washers fell to their deaths from the thirty-second floor of the hotel. A line securing their work platform snapped. The cause of the break in the line is unknown. Witnesses to the tragedy say the victims were caught totally off guard. One moment the platform was stable – the next the people were plunging to their deaths. No one on the ground was injured. Only one victim's name has been released at this point – Jene Roe, a twenty-eight-year-old mother of two children. Mrs Roe was the only female window washer in the entire city of San Francisco. Our own news correspondent, Stan Adams, was on hand in San Francisco to speak with Mrs Roe's husband about the accident. We move now to that interview.'

What followed was the media at its most pathetic. Mrs Roe's husband spent the majority of the interview sobbing while the reporter kept pounding him with the most inane questions. How does it feel to have your wife crushed on the pavement? Are you going to sue the city? How will your children grow up without a mother? Did Jene ever express the belief that she would die young? Poor Mr Roe didn't know what to say, except, 'God, why did this have to happen?'

It made me stop to think.

Indeed, why?

It hadn't happened yet. I could stop it.

I chided myself. How small my thoughts had been first to use the VCR to make money. Then I realised how good it was I had some extra cash. It was half past seven in the morning. I couldn't get to San Francisco by car by noon but I could fly. How exciting this was! I could save these people! I could save Mr Roe and his children years of pain. Jumping up from my bed, I called the airlines, made a reservation on a flight that was leaving at nine thirty and arriving in San Francisco at ten thirty. Then I got dressed. I kissed my father goodbye before I left the house.

'You were out late last night,' he said.

'Sorry. I've got your money for you.'

'I said it was yours.' He stood up from his place at the table. He had been eating toast and jam – that's all he ever ate in the morning. I liked Cheerios, with lots of milk. 'Are you all right, Rela?'

'Yes. But I'm in a hurry right now.'

'Where are you going?'

I paused. 'San Francisco.'

'*What?*'

'I'm flying up. I'll be back this evening, I promise.' I opened the door. 'You don't have to worry about me.'

'I do worry about you.' He took a step closer, paused, uncertain what to say. Our eyes met and he tried to smile but ended up shrugging and staring at the floor. 'It's just that I've never had a daughter before. I don't know if I'm doing right by you.'

'What do you mean? You're wonderful.'

He met my eyes again. 'I think you know what I mean.'

I shook my head faintly. 'No.'

He sighed. 'We should spend more time trying to find your family.'

I stiffened. 'That's not necessary.'

'Rela.'

'I'm sorry, I have to go. We can talk later.'

He took another step towards me, reached out, and touched my arm. 'What's in San Francisco?' he asked.

'No one I know.' I kissed him once more. 'Goodbye, Father.'

He held on to me a moment and hugged me. 'Goodbye, Rela.'

My flight was cancelled because of engine trouble. There was another flight thirty minutes later, the gentleman at the desk said. I got the ten o'clock one. The half hour delay was hard on me, though. When the plane landed in San Francisco I dashed out of the airport and jumped into a cab.

'The Hyatt,' I told the driver. 'Downtown.'

'Which one?' he asked.

'There are two? Damn. Are they both tall?'

He was a foreigner, maybe from India. He scratched his head. 'One is tall. One not so tall. They are both very nice.'

'Take me to the taller one.' My watch read eleven fifteen. 'How long will it take to get there?'

70

'Thirty to forty minutes.'

I didn't even know if the accident happened precisely at twelve. What if it was a quarter to twelve? I would be on time to see them covering the bodies. I opened my purse, choked with hundred dollar bills, and tossed one over the seat to the driver.

'I will give you another one of those when we reach the hotel if you run every red traffic light along the way,' I said.

The driver smiled and pocketed the money. 'In my country we always run the lights.'

He drove his cab like a roller coaster on a downhill spiral and really earned his extra hundred. After climbing out of the cab, I paused at the bottom of the steps of the hotel and leaned back to see a team of window washers working at what could have been the thirty-second floor. The time was ten minutes to twelve.

Now what was I supposed to do? I had rushed to the hotel as fast as I could but hadn't formulated a plan of action. As I jogged into the lobby, I saw an assistant manager's desk manned by a girl who didn't look much older than I was. Out of breath, I hurried up to her.

'The scaffolding that supports the window washers is giving way,' I blurted out.

She blinked. 'What? Who are you?'

'Nobody.' I pointed outside. 'I tell you the window washers are about to fall. Where do they secure their ropes when they're working?'

The young woman stood. She had been drinking a cup of coffee and accidentally knocked it over as she got up. She sopped up the mess with tissues, saying, 'They work from the roof down. How do you know their equipment is weakening?'

I saw it with my own eyes!'

She left her coffee and came round her desk. 'I must see for myself.'

'We don't have time for that!' I grabbed her by the shoulders and spun her towards me. I can only imagine how crazy I must have looked to her. Yet I was unable to control myself. 'Send a man to the roof immediately! They're going to die any minute!'

The young woman was indecisive. 'You say that from the outside you can see the scaffolding shaking?'

'Yes! It's giving way this very second!'

She reached down and picked up the phone on her desk. 'The window washers are not employees of the hotel, but I will have someone on our maintenance staff look into this matter.'

I backed away from the assistant manager. 'Tell them it's an extreme emergency.' Turning, I ran to the elevator. I did not trust that someone would get to the roof in the next few minutes. I didn't even know what I could do on the roof. As the elevator doors closed on me, I wondered if I'd find someone cutting the window washers' ropes, if the murderer would turn on me with his knife when he was done with the others and slit my throat.

That wasn't what happened. But before I could even get to the roof and see what the situation was, I had to find a way up there. The elevator only went to the top floor of the hotel, or rather, to the top floor where the guests stayed. I got off on that floor, number thirty-four, and frantically prowled up and down the hallways until I located what looked like a storeroom. It was unlocked, filled with vents and ducts and diesel motors. At the back, in the corner, was a steel ladder that led straight up. I went up the ladder two rungs at a time.

The wind on the roof was incredible. It blew my mind that normal people could be out cleaning windows so high up on such a turbulent day. Then I remembered that San Francisco was always windy. The roof was made of gravel embedded in tar. In the centre of it was a low white platform that supported a gigantic satellite dish. A wall of tan steel approximately four feet high ringed the entire roof. I was the only one up there.

Hurrying up and down the halls of the hotel had upset my sense of direction. I ran to what I believed was the right side and didn't see the window washers. I decided I was too late. Then I saw I was at the back of the hotel, and the people had been working at the front. I turned and ran to the other side. There they were, three storeys below me, happily working away to music from a boom box they had set up on the scaffold beside them. I saw Jene Roe. She was laughing at some joke.

Their ropes were secured in six places to thick metal hooks that protruded from the edge of the narrow wall that ringed the roof. A glance at the lines revealed no critical signs of wear, although the ropes were without exception old and dirty. I assumed the weakness was further down on the lines, perhaps where they were attached to the scaffold. The time was five minutes after twelve. I wasn't about to climb down it. I leaned over the edge.

'Hey,' I called. They looked up, all four of them. 'There's a call for Mrs Roe. It's from her husband. It's an emergency.'

It worked like a charm. Jene Roe put down her soapy wiper and climbed up the rope ladder. Now all I had to do was convince the other three there was an emergency at hand. I thought maybe Jene could help me out.

I must have been out of my mind. Naturally, when she came over the lip of the roof, she was anxious. She was a surprisingly attractive woman: blonde, voluptuous, with pouty red lips and green eyes. Why she was washing windows thirty storeys above the ground made no sense to me.

'Where's the phone?' she asked.

'Downstairs.'

'Do you know what the emergency is?' she asked.

'Your husband didn't say. Wait!' I grabbed her arm as she started to move past me. 'Your fellow workers have to come up right now, too.'

She stopped. 'Why?'

'Well, there's an assassin poised on a skyscraper over there.' I nodded and continued, 'And the police are afraid he's going to shoot. He hates window washers.'

Jene stared at me suspiciously and I didn't blame her one bit. 'Who are you? Do you work for the hotel?'

'Yes.'

'You look kind of young?'

'I'm older than I look.'

'Did my husband call and say there was an emergency?'

I hesitated. 'No. It's something else. It's that platform you're working on. It's going to fall.'

Now Jene was angry. 'You dragged me up here to tell me that?'

'Yes. I'm trying to save your life. Listen to me!'

Jene turned while I was talking, as if to climb back down the rope ladder to return to work. Later, I decided that hadn't been her intention. She was probably going to alert the others that there was a kook on the roof and that they might want to secure their lines elsewhere. I shouldn't have tried to stop her. But I realised that only in retrospect. At the time all I could think of was Mr Roe sobbing over his dead wife and how that very wife was about to climb back into danger. If I was too late to save the others, I thought, at least I would save her.

74

Jene had on a pair of baggy white pants, much like those of a house painter, and in one of her oversize pockets was a heavy black flashlight. Jene turned to protest. It was then I hit her over the head.

The blow was solid. She dropped to her knees and I whacked her again on the side of the head. That put her out. I felt sort of bad about it, but I was, after all, trying to save her life. My guilt did not stay with me long. From over the side of the roof I suddenly heard a loud *thump* and then heartrending screams.

I didn't want to look. I shouldn't have. But I did and what I saw was the end of three lives. The newscaster had been right. The platform had given way without warning. Not a single one of them had a chance to grab on to the lines, even to hang on for a second. It happened fast, yet they seemed to fall in slow motion, like puppets in the wind, their clothes puffed out big with rushing air. Their screams seemed to go on for ever. Even when they hit the concrete and the red exploded around their bodies, I still heard the screams. I closed my eyes and still saw the blood.

I left quickly. I knew I had to. I was no fool. When Jene regained consciousness she would blame me for the accident, even though I had done nothing but save her life. I was back down the ladder and into the elevator before anybody appeared. I left the hotel by the back door. A crowd had already gathered out front. I wondered what the assistant manager would tell the police.

I walked a couple miles from the hotel before I caught a cab. The driver – he was from Iran – had heard about the accident on the radio and wanted to talk about it, but I wasn't in the mood. It was still early in the afternoon when I reached the airport, but I couldn't get a flight back to L.A. until six in the evening. It wouldn't get in until seven. It was after eight when I got home and it was only then I remembered that I was supposed to have gone out with Christopher that night. There were two messages from him on our answering machine, one asking when he should come over and the other, apparently, placed after he had come to the house and found no one around. I called him briefly and told him that I had got tied up and I was sorry and that I wasn't feeling well and I would please talk to him the next day. He was sweet about the whole thing. He said sure.

My father was out. He had left a note that he'd be working late. I curled up on my bed in front of the TV with a glass of milk and turned on – what else – the current news. I didn't watch it long. The window washer accident was the top story. There were interviews with both Jene Roe and Ms Assistant Manager. Neither had a favourable opinion of me. Yes, big surprise, the police were actively searching for me. I was concerned, but only slightly. If the cabbie who had taken me to the hotel spoke to the police they'd know I had flown into the city. As a precaution against such a possibility I had not given my real name when I booked my ticket. They wouldn't find me, I decided.

Besides, if they did, I would see it on the news beforehand and be out when they came for me. I laughed at the irony of it.

Then I began to weep. I had never seen people die before. I had saved a life, I knew, but I should have saved all their lives. This VCR was a gift, but it was also a curse. If I kept taping tomorrow's news I knew I would be insane from the burden of it all. Because each day I would know where tragedy was to strike, and if I didn't prevent it, I would become a part of that tragedy. It gave me small comfort that Mr Roe had not been interviewed this time.

What an expression – *this time*. What had become of the *other* time? By saving Jene Roe, had I for ever altered the course of the world? What was I doing anyway? I wasn't God. I couldn't decide who lived and who died. Why was this happening to me? This will sound pathetic, but I hadn't stopped to ask myself these or any questions. I had been having too much fun enjoying my new toy. I hadn't paused long enough to think through why it was that I should buy a VCR that could see into the future. Of course, I had marvelled at the machine. I had said to myself again and again that it made no sense that it should work the way it did. But I hadn't really confronted the issue. I hadn't wanted to face the questions. Especially the most obvious of them all.

When did the VCR tape the future?

When exactly?

Downstairs, someone knocked on the front door.

Except for the light in my bedroom, the house was dark. I crept slowly down the stairs. The day's events had spooked me, and I was afraid to answer the door. I knew it was locked and no one could just walk in.

'Hello?' I called from the bottom step.

The person didn't say anything. He just knocked again.

'Who is it?' I called a little louder.

There was a lengthy pause. I was sure he'd heard me. He obviously didn't want to identify himself. This wasn't good, I thought. My father was a minister and wouldn't have a gun in the house. I didn't want to call the police. The police were searching for me.

The person knocked a third time.

I fought to keep my voice steady. 'Ed,' I said, pretending to call to someone in another room. 'Why don't you see who's at the door?'

I waited without moving, without breathing. Then, just when I felt I could wait no longer, when I thought I must cry out, I saw headlights move across the closed drapes. I recognised the sound of my father's truck. I listened as he parked and walked up to the door – I knew the sound of his steps. A moment later he was unlocking the front door and stepping inside. Relief flooded over me. I leapt off the last step and gave him a hug.

'Rela,' he said with enthusiasm. 'I'm happy to see you, too.'

I squeezed him tight. 'I'm so happy to see you.'

He must have noticed my fright. 'What's wrong?'

I let go of him. 'There was someone at the door. He was there just before you arrived. Didn't you see him?'

'No.'

'He was there just a few seconds ago.'

'There was no one.'

I shook my head. 'He must have run off when he saw you drive up.'

'That's odd. Did you see him?'

'No. He just knocked.'

'How do you know it was a he?'

I paused. 'It could have been a she.'

'Should we call the police?'

'No.' I hugged him again briefly. 'I'm safe now that you're home.'

'Did you go to San Francisco?'

I hated lying to him, but I didn't want him to read the paper and think of me in the city at the same time the people fell to their death. 'No,' I said. 'I went to the beach.'

He wasn't concerned that I had ditched school. 'Did you have fun?'

'It was a nice day.' I said.

TEN

In the dark, inside my dreams, I saw more. But I understood less.

I awoke from the operation to emptiness. I tried to move but couldn't. My throat was swollen – I doubted if I could speak. I opened my eyes with great effort.

I was in a hospital bed, alone in a room crammed with sophisticated life-support equipment. Tubes dripping coloured fluids ran into every orifice in my body. The odour of rubbing alcohol was in the air. Then I remembered my spine being ripped from my body, my skull being sawed open. Yet I felt no pain. I felt hardly anything at all, really. I didn't know who I was and even that didn't bother me.

Time passed – days, perhaps. People dressed in white, men and women, with empty expressions and cold hands occasionally entered my room and readjusted the tubes and solutions flowing into my body. Sometimes they would roll me over, remove my gown, and wash me with soapy water. But they didn't look at my eyes or speak to me. And I didn't speak to them. I had no words, no thoughts, nothing. I was just a mass of living tissue.

More time passed. There were no windows in the room, so day and night were one. There was no way to count the days. Soon the nameless people began to remove the tubes attached to my body, until eventually there were none left. They stretched my limbs, pulling my arms and legs this way and that. I let them do it. I didn't care about them, and I sensed they didn't care about me.

They made me get up and use the bathroom. They had begun to feed me solid food. I ate it without enjoying it. They had me walk around the room, back and forth. At first I could walk for only a few short minutes before my legs would ache and my heart would pound. But then I could exercise for longer and longer periods of time. The people who watched – sometimes there were two or three, sometimes only one – didn't act pleased and I didn't care if they were impressed or not.

Then, slowly, thought returned to my mind. Late at night, when the room was dark, I would awake to images of a young woman walking in the woods, singing. I would see her by the beach, playing in the waves. Most of all I would see her sitting beside an old man with white hair, talking late into the night. I didn't know who this young woman was, but I sensed that the old man was important. He was the cause of everything that was happening. Yet I didn't know what was happening.

And still I didn't care.

Until I remembered the purple vial of liquid.

Then I saw how *I*, the young woman, had injected myself with two vials of liquid, not one as I had imagined long ago in another place and time. There had been the green vial but first there had been the purple vial. It was the purple liquid that was supposed to preserve my memory.

The green liquid had been used to kill me.

Memory.

Part of it returned. My mission. My destiny.

The secrets of the universe. They were mine now.

But not my name.

I still didn't know who I was, even though I had begun to care.

I knew I had to escape. All because of the purple liquid. The purple vial.

I sat upon the edge of the bed and stared at the wall opposite me. The only door leading from the room was to my right and locked. I knew that without checking. But the door wasn't so important. I knew I could still get out. It was what was in the wall that mattered to me. It was what was in every bit of matter in the room, in every atom in the world . . .

The memory of everything that had ever been.

I stared at the wall, and as I did I felt myself merge with it. I saw the fine fragments of white plaster become magnified, no longer smooth as they appeared to the naked eye, but pitted and scarred with craters and ridges that took on gigantic proportions the farther I explored. Yes, I was probing the wall for the ultimate element. I knew I could find it here.

I pushed deeper. The plaster vanished and I saw the molecules that composed the materials of the wall, carbon atoms interlinked with oxygen and hydrogen to form substances that mankind had used since the dawn of civilisation. Right then I thought of all the people beyond the walls of the building I was trapped in. Emotion momentarily disrupted my plunge into the material. But I pushed it away because it was for the people of the world I had done what I had done. There was no need for sorrow. It mattered only that I had succeeded.

The molecules gave way to the interior of individual atoms. Electrons pulsed around me, neutrons and protons pulled me forward through a crack in reality where all emotion was left behind. I burst through to the nucleus of the atom and saw raw energy burning. Yet I knew even that great fire was only a ghost image imposed on the background of something more permanent. I flew past the smallest subatomic particle into a vast realm of black space. Space could never be conquered, I knew. It could never age. The universe was almost but not quite empty. It was permeated by immortal space.

And because of that I was also immortal.

I arrived at a place known as eternity.

A glance over my shoulder easily showed my creation. I stood at the centre of the wheel of creation, and every inch of the rim was visible simultaneously. A turn and I was brought to where it had all started. The wonder of it all was the endless paradox. I was bigger than the biggest, smaller than the smallest.

There was nothing in the beginning except a point, incredibly dense, incredibly tiny. All around was only emptiness. For aeons I observed the point, but because there was no time, the aeons passed in a flash. Then there was an explosion of light devoid of sound. A trillion times a trillion subatomic particles were created and destroyed in an instant. Energy flew in every direction. Fifteen billion years in the future, creatures called men on an insignificant planet orbiting an ordinary star would call this the Big Bang.

Now there was Time. And much of Time passed before the energy cooled sufficiently to form matter. I was coming back the way I had set off, but I didn't want to return to where I had started. I waited and watched, and finally that one ordinary star formed, and around it spun that one insignificant planet. Home. I knew this was where I belonged. Again I waited and watched and I remembered everything I saw. Life appearing, flourishing, changing, creeping up from the oceans, flying through the air, walking upright, and finally becoming conscious of *I*.

But who was this *I*?

Empty space, of course. The supreme element. Immortal.

But anything else?

The question that only the most delicate of feeling could answer.

I saw all of history, but I stopped before the final days of man. I didn't want to see them because I already knew the bitterness of the end.

I had been told about it.

I sat upright in bed and a faint moan escaped from my lips. The light in my room was on, even though I could vividly remember having turned it off. Anxious, I glanced around, but I was alone. My head fell into my hands and I felt my pulse pounding at my temples.

'I cannot keep having these dreams,' I whispered to myself. 'I will go insane if I do.'

Across the room, on top of my TV, a tape in my VCR made a faint clicking sound. The machine had been taping while I slept. Strangely enough, I couldn't remember if I had programmed it to tape before I went to bed.

I reached for the remote control.

The machine had taped the news two days hence.

Thursday night's programme.

The top story that night—

Was me.

A picture my father had taken of me two weeks earlier appeared in the upper left-hand corner of the screen beside the male announcer. My hair was loose over my shoulders and I was smiling. The man spoke with trained professionalism.

'The mutilated remains of eighteen-year-old Rela Lindquist were found this morning in the home of her adopted father, the Reverend Spencer Lindquist. Police

83

who first arrived at the scene said that it appeared as if her body had been torn apart by a psychotic with a saw and hammer. An autopsy is under way to pinpoint the exact cause of death. Mr Lindquist reported that his daughter had spoken of a stranger hanging around their house when he wasn't home a few days prior to her death. So far the police have arrested no suspects in connection with this crime. The last person to see Rela alive was her boyfriend Christopher Perry, a fellow student at Grover High. He also reported that Rela was upset about a man who'd been following her, but he was unable to provide a description of the individual, except to say that Rela said he looked familiar . . .'

I didn't shake. I didn't even cry. When my story was finished, I calmly reached for the remote control and turned off the VCR and TV. The truth of the matter was, I wasn't surprised. What else could be the result of tampering with the news except to become a part of the news? Or more precisely, I thought, I had upset destiny and in so doing I had pissed off fate. The Grim Reaper probably had a quota he collected each day. Since I had snatched Jene Roe from him he no doubt felt justified in coming for me.

The mutilated remains of Rela.

A strange man who looked familiar.

Now at least I knew who had been knocking at my door.

My murderer.

My calm didn't last long.

'All right,' I told myself. 'I know I won't die during the day. Dad will find me in the morning. That means I'm probably supposed to die tomorrow night sometime, so I'm totally safe for now. I know that. And I can use that to my advantage. Whoever's going to kill me doesn't know I know.'

But was that true? Maybe the real owner of the VCR had turned up. Maybe he had another crystal ball. Not so sophisticated as what I had. No four heads on his that would allow him to see everything in slow motion, but every bit as useful if he kept his ears close to the speakers and regularly made tapes. Then, if he knew what I knew, he would also know when to catch me alone and rip my guts out.

Maybe. There were still plenty of maybes left. And whys.

'Why would he need to disfigure me so?' I wondered out loud.

The time was three in the morning. I could do nothing now, I decided. I would make my plans later in the morning. I would talk to Christopher, explain what was happening, buy an M16 and fly to Australia if I had to.

'I'm not going to die,' I swore out loud as I reached over and turned off the light. 'That man is going to get it before I do.'

Surprisingly, I was asleep in minutes.

My dreams resumed almost immediately.

I wandered the streets alone. It was a summer evening, and the sun had yet to set, but my clothing was flimsy and there was a breeze. I shivered as the air swept my bare legs. I was in a busy city, I knew that much, and I had to find food and shelter. Those were my primary concerns. The light at the beginning of creation was forgotten. The bitter fate of the world was a bad dream I didn't quite believe. But at least I knew I was a young woman again. That was precious to me above all else.

I wandered about for hours. The sun vanished and it grew colder. The bloodshot eyes of the homeless swam before me. One street led to another – they all looked the same. I smelt the garbage of the city and then I began to smell like the garbage. I felt numb, hungry, exhausted – like an animal that had been stirred out of hibernation.

Finally I came to a busy corner and a middle-aged man in a blue business suit stared at me as if I were in trouble, which was an astute observation on his part. I had on only a green hospital gown.

'Can I help you?' he asked.

'I don't know. Where am I?' These were my first words.

'At the corner of Lake and Colorado.'

'What city?'

The man was concerned. 'Pasadena.'

'Where's that? What part of the country?'

'Pasadena is a suburb of Los Angeles.' He took a step closer and offered his free hand. He carried a briefcase in the other. I shook his hand and it was good to feel the warmth of his fingers. It had been a long time since I had touched anyone warm. 'My name is Paul Dorado. My car is nearby. Is there some place I can take you?'

I searched what was left of my tattered ruin of a memory. I saw more stars than people, felt closer to glaciers sweeping the world than to the cars driving by. But his mention of Los Angeles reassured me. I was in the right place. Now I just had to find – What did I have to find? I couldn't even remember if it was a person or a place or an object. I lowered my head.

'I don't know,' I said.

He put his hand on my shoulder. He was a nice man, I could tell. 'What's your name, girl?' he asked.

My eyes were moist. I did not want to look up and meet his gaze. I said the first thing that came into my head. 'I am Rela.'

'Rela? Is that it? Rela?'

86

The word did not sound pleasant, yet it resonated inside me. There was truth in the word. I raised my head and nodded. 'I am Rela. I do need help. I'm – lost.'

'Where are your parents?'

I gestured helplessly. 'Lost.'

'Where?'

I felt tears. 'I don't know where.'

He hugged my shoulder. 'You'll be OK, Rela. I know a place nearby to take you. It's a shelter where many people go when they've lost their homes. You can rest there and get back on your feet. The man who runs the place is a minister friend of mine.' He laughed. 'I think the first thing he has to do for you is get you some decent clothes. You look like you just got out of a hospital.'

'It was not a hospital,' I muttered as I let him lead me towards his car. 'It was a morgue.'

ELEVEN

Wednesday, the supposed last day of my life, I woke up late. The time was close to twelve noon when I rolled over in bed and checked the clock. I wasn't totally surprised. Actually, considering all the weird places I was travelling in my nightmares, I was surprised it wasn't Thursday morning already.

Yet I didn't fully remember the details of my dreams right then. I couldn't recall how Paul Dorado had taken me to the mission where I had met my father. The amnesia factor was still in effect, and that was not so strange because dreams, no matter how provocative, were still dreams. I was still hours away from realising I *was* a nameless orphan who had been found wandering the streets of Pasadena wearing a hospital gown. I wasn't asking myself the biggest questions of all.

Who was I?

Where had I come from?

I glanced at the VCR as I made my way to the bathroom. I didn't stop to see if there was more good news to enjoy. In fact, I reached over and unplugged the machine. It was a miracle, considering the grief I'd experienced since I had bought it, that I didn't toss the VCR out of the window. Of course, I realised, I might need it later to see if I was still to be a news item.

I repeated my vow from the previous night not to be caught unawares by my assailant. I debated going to school, then discarded the idea. Christopher would be there, but I wouldn't be able to convince him of the reality of what was happening unless I showed him the video tape. I would have to wait until after school, then, and go to his home with the latest tape, which chronicled my death.

I showered and dressed. Downstairs I found a note from my father. He said that I sure was a sleepyhead and that he hoped I had a nice day. It would kill him to find me dead, I knew. They would interview him and ask what it felt like to lose a daughter he had known for only three months. Then they would inquire how his God could let such a thing happen.

But they would not ask why God had selected me, of all people, eighteen-year-old Rela, to change what was to be? Vaguely, I remembered something from my unconscious excursions about destiny and mankind. But those thoughts, like the others, could not be comprehended in a waking state any more than the images of the beginning of time could be accepted by the rational mind. Yet I did faintly remember the brilliant light that erupted from the tiny point. In the midst of the horror had been great and profound beauty. Awe, even, that came close to inspiring in me the mysticism that Christopher so distrusted. Briefly, I wondered if he was the best person to confide in. Twice I had tried and twice I had choked up.

Did my subconscious know something my VCR did not?

I left the house and drove to the mall. I wanted to be where there were people. Along the way I kept glancing in the rear-view mirror for a shadow. But if my would-be murderer was following, he was shrewd and didn't give himself away. Yet, according to the tape, I was to meet my assailant before he killed me, and recognise him enough to describe him to Christopher as familiar.

'Well,' I said out loud in the car, 'if I run into someone who fits that description I will just knife him on the spot.'

The first thing I did when I reached the mall was buy a big Swiss Army knife. Then I got myself a Häagen-Dazs vanilla milk shake and sat at the centre of the mall and watched as people enjoyed an idyllic afternoon of shopping and browsing. I had twenty thousand dollars in my purse and couldn't think of anything I really wanted to buy except a twelve-gauge shotgun. The manager of the sporting goods store told me he wouldn't sell me one unless he saw I.D. I wondered if I should try to bribe him.

Two o'clock came and I figured Christopher should be home. I drove to his house without calling. There was no one there. Anxious about the passing hours and my lack of a clear plan, I considered my choices. I couldn't leave the country because I didn't have a passport. But I could leave the state. I could drive to the airport this minute and take a plane to Hawaii. I could go to a dozen different places. Yet I had to wonder if the fleeing strategy was entirely useful.

Who was supposed to kill me? It had to be someone connected to what was happening with the VCR, or else I was having the most coincidentally bad week a teenager could have. This person – I finally decided – this man, *must* have access to the same information I had. Given that fact I couldn't defeat him by running. He would find me, probably away from what few friends I had. I could only face him tonight armed in such a way that he couldn't anticipate it with a time machine of any make or model. Yeah, it sounded logical but I didn't like the sound of it any more than I liked the sound of my own name.

'Rela,' I said aloud. The word disturbed me – all of a sudden.

I went to work at the library. I know that sounds crazy but I didn't know where else to go. Besides, at the library I was constantly surrounded by people. And I loved my job, surrounded by so many books, so many lives, so much of the past. The history section was always my favourite to browse in whenever I had a spare minute. It was therefore no major coincidence that at about six o'clock, three hours before closing, I was standing in the history section flipping through the pages of a book on the Civil War when a bald man in a tight grey tracksuit approached me.

'Hello,' he said kindly. 'Can you help me?'

I looked at him and didn't immediately pee my pants. My anxiety was growing by the minute, though, make no mistake. I had been unable to get Christopher on the phone all evening. The man didn't look familiar at first. Indeed, he appeared to be like no one I had ever seen before. His clothes were different; if it was a tracksuit it was not cut like any in the stores. It had no seams. His grey eyes were odd – they were unusually bright. I blinked as I stared into them and then hastily closed the Civil War book I was holding.

'Yes,' I said. 'What are you looking for?'

His lips moved into a smile, although his eyes remained untouched by the warmth of it. He pointed at the book I was holding. 'I am looking for a book on the Civil War,' he said. 'Isn't that a coincidence?' He tugged lightly on my book. 'May I?'

'Yes, of course.' I let him take the book and watched as he opened to the first page. 'It's one of the better ones,' I added.

'Is it accurate?' he asked.

'No.'

He was interested. 'Why do you say that?'

I shrugged. 'I mean, it's as accurate as you can get. But I think you'd have to have been alive at that time really to get a feel for the war.'

'Doesn't this book quote from letters and speeches that were written by people who lived in those times?' he asked.

'You've read this book, then?'

'No, I haven't. Have you?'

I realised that I hadn't. Suddenly I didn't like this man. His eyes – they were so bright they could have been electrified. Fear – faint, but nevertheless real – entered my mind. Could this be the one?

But he didn't look familiar. He just looked weird.

'I've glanced through it,' I said, suddenly looking past him. 'Excuse me, if you don't need any other help, I have to get back to work.'

As I stepped by him he said, 'But if I do need help, you will be here?'

'I'll be around,' I muttered, not facing him.

I spent the rest of the evening in the back sorting magazines and trying to get Christopher on the phone. Finally his mother picked up. She said he wouldn't be home till nine, which was exactly when I got off. It was madness, I know, working for a few measly dollars an hour while my life steadily slipped away. I kept peeking out from the back to see if the bald man had left. He had taken a seat near the front – he could see everyone who was coming and going – and was reading the Civil War book I had recommended. It looked like he would stay to closing. I noticed he had a medium-size black suitcase resting on the floor beside him.

By ten minutes to nine I was desperate. I'd even tried Stacy a couple of times but had been unable to reach her, too. I thought of Ed and got the number for Circuit City from Information. I caught him at work.

'Ed,' I said. 'This is Rela. Remember me?'

'Hey, yeah. How are you? Great to hear from you. Thanks for introducing me to your pal. She's something – you never know what's going to come out of that girl's mouth.'

'You two are seeing each other?'

'Yeah, didn't she tell you? I guess she didn't want to break your heart. How are you doing, Rela? How's your new VCR treating you?'

'Let's just say it's changed my life in dramatic ways.' I lowered my voice. 'Ed, I'm in trouble and I mean serious trouble.'

'You're pregnant?'

'No. I have someone following me. I'm at work right now, and I'm not sure, but I think he may be here, waiting for me to walk out to my car.'

'Get someone to walk out with you.'

'I'm going to do that. But then I have to drive home to an empty house. It's Wednesday and my father always works late on Wednesday. He helps pass out food at the mission. Often he sleeps there and doesn't come home till morning.'

'Can't you call him at the mission?'

'I don't want to bother him.' Actually I didn't want to get him involved, maybe get him killed, although according to the TV news that appeared unlikely. 'Ed, could you do me a favour? Could you go to my house and be there when I get home?'

'When are you going to get home?' he asked.

'I leave here in about ten minutes, and my house is only ten minutes away. I can hang around a few minutes longer while the head librarian closes up, but that doesn't take her long.'

Ed sighed. 'You would have to ask tonight of all nights. I have to be here till ten. I'm supposed to close up. Look, why don't you call the police?'

'I can't.'

'Why not?'

'I can't explain to them why I know this man is dangerous. They wouldn't believe me. But he is extremely dangerous. You've got to believe me.'

'I do, I do,' he said quickly. 'I can tell you're serious. Have you had dealings with him in the past?'

'Yes. In a way.'

'Why do you have to drive home? Go to an all-night coffee shop like Denny's. There's one not far from my store, at Madison and Parker. I can meet you there immediately after work. Then we can talk about it.'

'That's an idea,' I said. Indeed, home was the worst possible place I could go because it was at my house that my mutilated remains were supposed to be found. 'I'll meet you there,' I said. 'But if I'm not there when you get off work then drive straight to my house.'

'Gotcha. Do you want me to stay the night?'

'If you could.'

Ed was surprised. 'You must be scared.'

We said our goodbyes and I set the phone down. Another glance out the door showed me the man still hadn't budged, even though the librarian, Mrs Garcia, had flickered the lights as a sign that people should soon complete their business. A few people moved to the counter to check out books. Mrs Garcia shook the bell on the counter. We were the only two on duty. She wanted me to help her take care of the people. The moment I stepped out from the back, the bald man in the grey tracksuit stood up and picked up his suitcase and stepped towards the counter with his book in his free hand. He told Mrs Garcia that he was new to the area and that he needed a library card. She directed him to me. Now I was ready to pee my pants. His Day-Glo eyes raked me up and down as he stepped in front of me. He set the book on the counter and removed his wallet from a back pocket.

'I have identification,' he said. His voice was incredibly dry.

'Good,' I mumbled, keeping my gaze down. He gave me a valid California driver's licence that had been reissued the previous month. His address was listed as 1357 North Spain Road, Pasadena. His name was Henry Glover, born November 22, 1945, in Los Angeles. I turned away. 'This will take me a couple of minutes,' I said.

'Take your time,' he said. 'I have time.'

I don't, I thought. While making up his library card, my eyes kept straying, not to him but to the picture on his licence. *It* looked familiar, and I didn't understand how that could be when it looked like him and he seemed so foreign to me. The mystery did nothing to put me at ease about him. With each passing second I became more and more convinced that I now knew the man who was supposed to kill me.

I finished with his card and returned to the counter to check out his book. He followed my every movement. I was so close to screaming it was a wonder I didn't set off the smoke alarms. When I was done, I turned away without looking up.

'Thank you for your help,' he said.

'No problem,' I said softly.

I had to look up finally. It was almost as if he was challenging me to. I met his steady gaze. 'I'm Rela,' I said.

'That's a curious name. Rela. Quite beautiful.'

'Thank you – Henry,' I said.

95

He lifted his book and his black suitcase, which looked heavy but which he handled effortlessly. 'See you later,' he replied. Then he turned and left the library.

'Did you know that man?' Mrs Garcia asked, glancing over.

I swallowed thickly. I knew then that I needed to look no further for my assassin. 'He's an old friend,' I said.

Before I left the library with Mrs Garcia fifteen minutes later I got Christopher on the phone. He was beginning to explain why he had just come in when I interrupted.

'Can I come over?' I asked.

'When?'

'Now.'

'Now is not a good time. Both my mom and dad have the flu. If you come, you might catch it.'

'I don't care. I have to talk to you. I have a tape I have to show you—' I froze. I had not brought the tape with me. It was at home, in my machine, that accursed VCR.

'What does this tape have on it?' he asked.

'A copy of the news. Listen, I need to get that tape before I talk to you. But it's at my house, and I can't go to my house.'

'Why not?' he asked.

Once more I lowered my voice. 'A man has been following me. I believe he's waiting in the parking lot right now to follow me home. My father's not there. That's why I can't go there.'

Christopher was silent a moment. 'Are you serious?'

'Yes, this man is out there and he's after me. But please don't tell me to call the police. I can't and please don't ask me why. Just help me, OK?'

'Sure. Do you have someone to walk out with you?'

'Mrs Garcia. She's going to leave in a minute.'

96

'Then leave when she leaves, get in your car and immediately lock your doors. Drive straight here. Don't worry about my parents. They won't mind once I explain the situation to them.'

'But I need to get the video tape.'

'Forget the tape. We can get it tomorrow.'

'No. Tomorrow's no good. I can't talk to you about what's happening unless you watch the tape first. Believe me, you'll think I've lost my mind.'

'I can get the tape if it's so important to you. I can get it now and be back before you arrive.'

'No. The house is locked. I'll have to meet you there and give you the key.'

'Come here first and give me the key. You don't want this guy to know where you live.'

'Oh, he already knows that.' I figured he knew a lot of other things about me, maybe more than I knew myself. I continued, 'Time is critical here. I have to show you that tape as soon as possible. Meet me at my house. You're closer to it than I am. If you leave now, you'll be there before me. This man will do nothing while you're around.'

'How can you be so sure?' he asked.

I don't even know where the words came from. I just blurted them out. 'Because you're too important.'

TWELVE

The library parking lot was empty when we went outside. Mrs Garcia sensed I was upset about something but I didn't confide in her. I practically ran to my car when I saw the coast was clear. But I didn't climb inside until I checked twice that the back seat was empty. I had seen a horror film or two in my day.

Christopher was waiting on my porch when I drove up. He stood and hugged me as I got out of my car. 'Is he following you?' he asked.

'I don't know. I didn't see him. But that doesn't mean anything with this guy.'

'Who is he?' Christopher asked.

I hurried towards the front door. 'I don't know his real name. He goes by fake ones. But he's dangerous.' I aimed the key at the lock and had to use both hands to get it in the hole. 'He's killed before.'

Christopher was astounded. 'This is ridiculous, Rela. If he really is following you, you must go to the police.'

I gave him a sharp look. 'Do you think for a moment I made this guy up?'

Christopher was not flustered. 'No. All I'm saying is that you may not have a clear idea of what he wants from you. Let's call the police and let them assess the situation.'

I slammed my fists into my sides in frustration. 'I told

you I can't go to the police! We are dealing here with a force beyond anything they know!'

Christopher took a step back. 'What kind of force?' he asked.

I turned back to the keyhole. 'You'll have to see the tape. I want you to look at it now, here, before you do anything else. The man will not come while you're here.'

'You don't know that,' he protested.

'It's one of the few things I do know.'

We went inside and locked the door behind us. Christopher made a quick check of the first floor of the house to see that no one was there. I ran upstairs to get my VCR. My bedroom light was on, which surprised me. I hadn't left it on when I went out of the house.

Or had I? Last night when I awakened, the light had also been on, even though I remembered turning it off when I went to bed. Then, at three in the morning, I had watched the tape describing my gruesome death. Afterwards I had turned off the light and gone back to sleep and dreamt of wandering the streets of Pasadena half naked.

Yet if I had got up in the night again and turned on the light, I might not have noticed it in the light of day.

'But why would I have got up and turned on the light?' I asked myself.

For the same reason I got up and turned it on before?

Yes, I remembered now how the light had been on at least once before when I awakened from a nightmare, not just the night before. But I wasn't answering my own question. I had been sleepwalking – the bathtub incident proved that – but what was my need for light?

Was I doing *something* during the night?

I studied the VCR. The plug dangled from the back of it; the machine was off. I hadn't checked the tape that afternoon when I got up because I felt I'd already seen enough bad news. Plus I had not reset the VCR after viewing my death story. There should have been nothing new on the news.

Yet – my bedroom light was on. I must have turned it on again after turning it off. I must have been up one more time during the night.

I decided I should have another glance at the tape.

Before I showed it to Christopher.

I stepped to my bedroom door and called down to him. 'I have to use the bathroom. I'll be down in a minute.'

'OK,' he called up.

I closed the door and plugged the VCR in and settled in front of the TV with my remote control in hand. I didn't rewind the tape. I started it where I'd left off, immediately after the story of eighteen-year-old Rela Lindquist's mutilation. I pressed the Play button. The same male announcer who had read the piece about my murder came on.

'Good evening,' he said. 'Our top story tonight—'

'Oh, no,' I gasped.

I pressed the Pause button.

The news was on again. Thursday night's – the same news *starting over from the beginning.* Only it wasn't the same because instead of my picture in the upper right-hand corner of the screen, they had Christopher's. Dead, I thought. Now they would get him instead of me. But I had to know for sure. Shaking, tears already welled in my eyes, I pressed the Play button again.

'In Pasadena the body of eighteen-year-old Christopher Perry was found this morning in the home of the Reverend Spencer Lindquist. It appears as if his neck was broken by a very strong man, police say. But an autopsy is now under way to determine the exact cause of death. Mr Lindquist reported that he spent the night working at a homeless mission and did not come home until approximately eight in the morning. Missing at this time is Mr Lindquist's adopted daughter, Rela Lindquist.' My picture replaced Christopher's. It was the same one they used for my mutilation. The newscaster continued. 'According to Mr Lindquist, Rela spoke of a stranger hanging around their house a couple days ago. It is assumed that Rela was abducted by the same person who killed Christopher. So far the police have arrested no one in connection with these crimes. Christopher's parents have reported that their son left the house at approximately nine the previous night to got to the aid of Rela, who had called from her job at the library complaining about being followed by a man. He didn't come home or call after that. Both Rela and Christopher were students at Grover High in Pasadena . . .'

I pressed the Stop button and leaned over and sobbed on my knees. My confusion was as great as my sorrow. I didn't understand how tomorrow's news could have so drastically changed in the space of a few hours. One moment I'm a goner and the next it's Christopher. What element had been altered in the scenario?

Of course, there was only one.

When the first news had been recorded I didn't know I was to die. Then, because I knew, someone else had died. I sat up with a jolt of realisation.

'I wouldn't have brought Christopher to my house tonight if I hadn't known I was supposed to get killed.' I said out loud.

That knowledge was the big change.

'Christopher!' I yelled as I unplugged the VCR and cradled it in my hands. He was halfway up the stairs when I opened my bedroom door. 'We have to get out of here,' I said.

'What's happened?' he asked.

'I'll explain later. You cannot stay in this house. The man might come here, after all.' I literally shoved him down the stairs. 'Come on, we don't have a second to lose.'

Christopher put his hand to his head. He was sweating profusely. 'Then why are you taking your VCR with you?'

'I need my VCR!'

'I have one at my house,' he said.

'Not like this one. Let's just go. Please, I'll explain in the car.'

We were in the living room, heading for the front door, when I noticed that the living room window was shut. My father was a fresh-air addict. He never closed that window, even when it was freezing outside. I set the VCR down on the coffee table in front of the sofa and checked on the window.

'Someone was here,' I muttered.

Christopher stood behind me. 'Are you sure?'

I tried to pull the window up. I was pretty strong, but I couldn't budge it. It was as if it had been nailed shut. 'I'm quite sure.' I stared off into space for a moment. 'Why would he want the windows shut?' I whirled around. 'Are you sure that there's no one in this house?'

'I checked every room except your bedroom.'

'There's no one in my bedroom.'

Christopher staggered slightly to the left. 'Then why are you suddenly so anxious to leave here?'

I pointed at the tape. 'It's because of what's on this tape.' I paused and eyed Christopher. 'You're breathing heavily. Do you feel all right?'

He put his hand to his head again. 'I'm fine.'

I took a step towards him. 'You don't look fine. What's wrong with you?'

He rubbed his eyes and staggered back. 'Dizzy. Maybe it's all this running around. Let's get outside in the fresh air.' He reached for the VCR. 'I'll take this.'

'No, I'll get it,' I said.

'It's no problem,' he said and smiled at me as he leaned over to pick it up. His face was soaked with perspiration. 'Did I ever tell you how cute you look when you're scared?'

I had to grin. 'No. That's sweet.'

He stretched forward and lightly kissed my lips. 'You're sweet, Rela.'

Then he collapsed, unconscious on the floor at my feet.

'Christopher!' I screamed.

Every light in the house went out.

'God,' I whispered.

In the dark, alone, which had never frightened me before because I could see so well in it. Better than anybody I knew. But this dark was unreal. It seemed to come from inside as much as from outside, emerging from history I couldn't remember. I stepped away from Christopher, trying to pierce the blackness in any direction, but seeing nothing. Listening intently, with hearing that was better than most people's, but hearing nothing. The same excellence could not be applied to my speech, however. I wanted to scream, to bring the neighbours running, but my throat was choked with terror; my voice was dying of asphyxiation. Also, I knew that man who had killed the lights must be just outside. I backed into the phone stand and almost knocked it over. I frantically picked up the phone.

There was no dialling tone.

103

My hand flew to my pocket.

I still had my Swiss Army knife.

Someone knocked on the front door.

'Jesus,' I whispered.

The door was locked. I did not have to answer it. Silently I scampered the couple steps back to where Christopher had fallen. I shook him hard and he moved like a bowl of Jell-O. 'Christopher!' I hissed. 'Wake up!'

He was out cold. And nobody had laid a hand on him.

The person knocked on the front door again.

I ran to the back door. It was locked from the inside, but even when I turned the catch it refused to open. I hadn't locked the man out; he had locked me in. It made no difference. There was no way I was going to leave unconscious Christopher to the mercy of the man.

I returned to the living room in time to hear the man knock a third time. I realised this could not go on for ever. I was trapped.

'Who is it?' I said softly, finding my voice.

There was a lengthy pause. Then a voice – not exactly the same as that of the man in the library, more familiar really, but I don't know if I was just listening differently – said, 'It's me, Rela. You have to let me in.'

I moved closer to the door. My trembling had ceased, although my heart continued to pound silently in my chest and like thunder in my head. I think I stopped breathing when Christopher collapsed and had yet to start again.

'Why do I have to do anything you want?' I whispered. Whoever was outside had excellent hearing as well. He heard me easily enough.

'There is nowhere for you to run,' he said.

'Why don't you just break the door down?' I asked. 'I know you're capable of it.'

'The less I do the better.'

I was close to the door now. 'If I let you in will you promise not to hurt Christopher?' I asked.

He didn't hesitate. 'That I can promise.'

A tear ran over my cheek. 'Will you hurt me?'

'I think we both know the answer to that, Rela.'

'Yes,' I mumbled, and a part of me did understand. Christopher was important. I was expendable. I had been tossed aside before. That was part of what my nightmares had been about. I reached out and unlocked the door and opened it. The man stood perfectly still on the dark porch; a statue carved from the night. Yet his eyes were so very bright. He carried his black suitcase in his left hand.

'May I come in?' he asked.

I stepped aside. 'Yes. Can I have the lights back on please?'

He nodded as he stepped by me, and made a flicking motion with his right hand. All over the house, the lights came on at once. Christopher lay facedown in front of the couch. The man glanced at him.

'He is unhurt?' he asked.

'I believe so. What did you do to him?'

'I gassed the interior of this house. The gas is dissipating as we speak.'

'Is that why all the windows were shut?'

'Yes,' he said.

'The gas didn't affect me.'

'No. It doesn't affect me either.'

'What's wrong with Christopher that it bothers him?'

The man was watching me. He had not changed out of his grey tracksuit. 'You are asking the wrong question.'

'I understand,' I said. It was we who were different. I gestured to a chair opposite the couch. The man sat down, his suitcase resting on the floor beside his left

105

knee. I wondered what was inside. I sat on a chair between the man and Christopher. My almost boyfriend appeared to be breathing easily. 'Will you be staying long?' I asked the man.

His expression was impassive. 'It will not take long.'

A shiver went through my body, but I kept my voice even. 'Who are you?'

'You know who I am.'

'Where are you from?'

'You know where I am from.'

I stopped. The pupils of his grey eyes were wide. Dark tunnels into an alien mind. 'Who am I?' I whispered.

'Wrong question, Rela.'

'I don't understand.' But I did, even before he reached out with his right hand for my left hand. I understood that there could be no happy ending for me because from the beginning I had been cursed. I gave him my hand freely, yet I flinched as his fingers encircled mine. 'Will it hurt?' I whimpered.

'There are many kinds of pain in this universe,' he said, tugging on the ring finger of my left hand, the one I had cut Saturday night at my party. I still had my bandage on, but he pulled that off in a second. Then – actually, this was very disturbing – he took off more than the white gauze. Leaning closer, I saw he was removing my skin. Yes, he was tearing it off bit by bit as if it were made of wax. The weird thing was I didn't feel any physical pain and there wasn't a lot of blood. But he was dead right about there being many kinds of pain in the universe. I felt a big one right then – one I had never experienced before – when I looked past where the skin had been removed from my finger and saw nothing but copper wires and silver metal. Nothing else.

Nothing living.

'*What* are you,' he corrected. 'That's the question.

You are a RELA. A *R*obotic *E*xperimentation *L*ogistical *A*lgorhythm. Once, in another time, you had another name.' I stared down at the mangled flesh of my finger, the uninjured circuitry, and didn't have to ask myself why I didn't weep. My tear ducts, I realised were just a switch that I chose not to throw.

'I see,' I whispered.

'Yes.' He removed something that resembled a ray gun from his back pocket and pointed it at me. 'I have to destroy you now, and even though it is not logical, it will give me a measure of satisfaction to know that you died with your memory intact.' He aimed the weapon at my hand. 'Do you remember the name Sara?'

I closed my eyes. The shock had broken through my amnesia. I felt the purple vial in my hand; I saw it. The secrets of the universe were mine for a second. Of course a robot could process a trillion bits of data in a single moment.

I remembered everything and it was no dream.

'Yes, Grandfather,' I said. 'It was you who named me.'

THIRTEEN

I was born in the year 2036 in a city that was known as Los Angeles. My family was relatively well-to-do, for the times, and when I was five, they were able to move out of the city, away from the smog. We went north of San Francisco to a little town called Humboldt. I grew up there in what was left of the redwood forest. The ocean water there, my mother told me, was special. We could walk freely along the shore without special protection. In time I would be able to swim in it, and that was something I longed to do. Huge purifying plants had been built, my mother explained, to clean the ocean and return it to the way it had been before men polluted it.

Often, between my sixth year and my tenth, my grandfather would come to visit us. He was famous, a Nobel Prize winner, but he always brought me toys and called me his favourite girl, which was good with me, even though I knew I was his only grandchild. Especially prized by me were the dolls he gave me. They could walk, talk, eat – do many things that I commanded. He built them himself in his laboratory – the government didn't know everything he did there. No one did, not even my mother.

Grandfather called himself Saint Nick because he liked to think of himself as Santa Claus. That was his ego speaking, I was told. But whatever it was, he was like Santa to me and he loved to spend time with me, talking about the stars, the trees, the sea. He taught me to play the piano, which he played wonderfully, and we'd go for long hikes into the hills in the morning and evening. Once he told me I reminded him of a girl he knew when he was young, but he never said the girl's name and his voice was sad when he spoke of her. I wondered if she had been his wife, my mother's mother, for I knew she had died not long after my mother was born. My mother told me it wasn't so, and she did not know the girl's name, either.

Then my grandfather left and didn't come back for a few years, although he called occasionally, always at holidays and on my birthday, and spoke to me. He also sent gifts, but they were from the stores and didn't compare to the dolls he made in his lab. When we spoke, he never told me what he was working on except to say that it was very important.

I grew into a teenager and good and bad things happened in the world, mainly bad. There was a war in Europe and nuclear bombs were used and many people died, and the news said Europe was like the Middle East, which was already a radioactive wasteland. But the war ended quickly, and most scientists believed little radiation would drift to our part of the globe. The reconstruction of Europe began – slowly.

The economy of the United American Countries plunged into deep depression, and thirty per cent of all people lost their jobs. Food lines were everywhere, and the farmers in the middle of the continent had little uncontaminated land to cultivate. Much of the food they did grow was contaminated, too, and people began to catch new strains of viruses that were resistant to medicine.

Finally there was an explosion at our lunar colony and in one blow the entire colony was wiped out. The government said it would give up on space travel for the remainder of the century.

These catastrophes touched my family only slightly. My father kept his job as an engineer at a factory that was developing new types of plastic, and we had money to buy black market food, better than that that was available in the government stores. I suspected, although I was never told and never had the nerve to ask, that my father's income was supplemented by cheques from my grandfather.

The single good thing to emerge from these times was a worldwide humanitarian agency similar to the United Nations but smaller and more influential in its scope. It was called New Life, and at its core was a group of dedicated men and women willing to tackle the problems of the world to make them better. The New Lifers were suddenly everywhere, in all sections of society, recruiting volunteers and soliciting money to rebuild humanity. They met with immediate success wherever they went. For example, their scientists – they had assembled a team of the most brilliant – tackled the problem of pesticide toxicity and in three short years discovered chemicals that would counteract the effects of decades of abuse from soil additives.

New Life took small African nations that had been bankrupt since the day their constitutions were signed and got them back on sound financial footing. Of all the places in the world, Africa accepted New Life's aid the quickest and benefited the most. It was not long before the rest of the world turned to this remarkable agency for inspiration.

But what exactly was this organisation? The media debated the question endlessly. On the surface New Life was simply thousands of people helping other people. But its centre was mysterious. Its board of directors had to be made up of extraordinarily wealthy and intelligent people. Yet these people, for the most part, chose to remain anonymous. On the other hand, and this was the paradox, this same group seemed able to influence whole governments to bend to New Life's own particular vision of what should be done next. It sounded dangerous, ominous, but it wasn't because New Life's intervention was always positive. Also there was the fact that New Life had no single leader, and this allayed many of the world governments' worst fears. It wasn't as if too much power could be concentrated in one person.

Or so it seemed until I was eighteen years old and my grandfather suddenly showed up at our doorstep.

He had aged twenty years in eight. His hair was now entirely white, what little there was of it. He had never been a solidly built man but now he was emaciated. The biggest change, though, was in his eyes. They had always been so forceful, so full of possibility, and now they looked like burned-out video tubes. He had come to the house one afternoon when my parents were out and slumped down on the couch beside me and smiled and asked how I was doing. I told him I was fine and put my hand on his lined forehead. It was then he began to shake and his eyes brimmed full of tears.

He did not, in that one afternoon, tell me everything about his involvement with New Life. But he was to spend the next six weeks at our house, slowly recovering his health. During that time I would come to understand why the new hope of mankind was in reality its most deadly foe. The revelations came out of him in the form of several long dialogues we had during his recovery, most of them late at night in the makeshift room my mother had put together for him in our basement. It may sound strange, that he would confide in me rather than in his own daughter. My grandfather had not seen me in eight years, yet he knew me. His genes had passed undiluted into me. He knew I had his intelligence, his creativity. Yet I think, perhaps, he also understood that I did not suffer his same fears.

Our first talk was a week after he came back home. He spoke to me of his first love, physics, and his search for the ultimate theory.

'Einstein was working on a unified field theory when he died,' he said. 'I'm sure you've read about it in your history and science books, Sara. Many scientists have worked on it since, but none with complete success. There are four basic forces in nature: electromagnetic forces, weak nuclear forces, strong nuclear forces, and gravitation. Of the four, gravitation has always been the most difficult to define in relation to the others. I believe that's because it's the most fundamental. Consider how the galaxies and stars and planets were formed. There were huge clouds of gas floating everywhere, but it was gravity that pulled them together, made them into something that gave rise to the other forces. Without gravity there would have been no nuclear fusion and without that, no stars would have lit up the vast reaches of space. It is fusion that produces light, and light that creates the thermodynamics of all systems. All chemical reactions on this planet can be traced back to gravity. The same with life itself.

'I wanted to develop the ultimate unified field theory that explains how everything is related to everything else. I believed – in ignorance or with insight – that I was destined to discover it. But in time, with failure upon failure, I came to the conclusion that no such theory could be propounded, considering our limited observations into the structure of matter. You might find that statement odd. I was a world-famous scientist. I had at my disposal the largest and most powerful atom accelerators, computers, telescopes, whatever, to prove or disprove any theory I could put forward. Yet I soon felt these instruments were useless in my search for truth.

'When the scientific age dawned, we began to probe matter, to discover what it was made of. Quickly we learned there were molecules and that these molecules were made up of atoms. Then we discovered that atoms were comprised of electrons and protons and neutrons, and then inside these were other subatomic particles, mesons, quarks, and so on. We kept developing more sophisticated instruments to take a peek at finer levels of creation, but no matter what level we uncovered, there was always a level beneath it. Who was to say, I thought one day, that there was not an endless succession of layers?

'I was primarily a physicist but I was intrigued by a substance that no physicist of my time was studying: thought. What thought was made of. It had to be made of something, I reasoned. We all experienced it. We talked about it endlessly. Our entire civilisation was a result of thought. Yet most physicists would have said thought was nothing, that it didn't exist in a quantitative fashion. Yet my thoughts of thought would not leave me, and I turned my full attention to the enigma of its origin.

'I began to examine the brain in earnest. What I discovered was that for all the progress neurology and related disciplines had made in mapping which parts of the brain affected which expressions of thought – emotions such as anger and lust, decision-making capacities and so forth – no one had explained what a thought was and no one knew if thought had anything to do with the external environment. This was an important issue to me. Did thought affect matter? Could it? I sought in vain to find one psychic who could bend a spoon in front of me. The more I explored the more it seemed there was the universe out there and our dreams locked up in here and never the two should *directly* meet. I emphasise the word *directly* because obviously our thoughts had changed our planet, and not always or even usually for the better. But could thought touch a tree? Could thought touch an atom? I wondered.

'A new area of science began to make itself strongly felt about this time. It was called genetic techno-engineering or, more simply, GTE. It was an offshoot of genetic engineering itself, which as you know experiments with life on the cellular level. GTE operated in a similar fashion but was dedicated to fusing biology and engineering. A student of GTE would ask the question, why should we just splice one gene to another? Why don't we stir in a few microchips? I think it would be safe to say GTE was the first attempt at merging the living with the non-living. The entire subject fascinated me and I pursued it along with all my other interests.

'But I didn't get any further with GTE than any other enthusiastic amateur might have until I met a man by the name of Arthur Hapshaw. He was probably the leading GTE man until ten years ago. He had successfully combined a crystalline computer chip with the genetic material of a monkey's fertilised egg – in a test tube. I am saying the foetus of the monkey was being grown in an artificial womb and that the microchip was directing the development. I see you are interested, Sara, in how the baby monkey turned out. Let me just say this: that monkey could beat most girls your age at a game of checkers.

'Hapshaw had improved one species of life by direct microtechnology intervention. You have probably already guessed the next step he wanted to take

114

– to experiment on a human foetus. Fortunately or unfortunately, the government would not allow him that freedom of action. So Frankenstein's monster was never born in Hapshaw's laboratory.

'Yet he had opened a door with his success. He had discovered that technology could directly affect intelligence and therefore thought itself. The government did give him permission to begin experiments on braindead patients. These were people – I am sure you can imagine their sorry state – who had been in accidents that had destroyed their higher brain functions but left them alive. Hapshaw cultured human brain tissue in test tubes and introduced his microchips on the cellular level to try to boost the energy and reproductive capabilities of the cells. He met with rapid success. Soon he was injecting the tissue samples directly into the cerebral cortices of patients who had been comatose for years. Then a miracle occurred. One of the patients woke up and began to speak. Then another, and another.

'I see I have a hundred per cent of your attention now, Sara. I can guess what you're thinking. Did the people who awoke become superhuman thinking machines? No, in fact, most of them remained somewhat slow, although a few regained normal mental capabilities. That shouldn't surprise you and it didn't surprise us. Oh, I forgot to mention that by this time I was working full-time with Hapshaw. Yes, it was a switch for me, from physics to GTE. But you know I was always interested in anything and everything and I don't think I'd be bragging to say that I have the equivalent of a doctorate in both chemistry and biology as well as in computer engineering.

'Anyway, we had only attempted to stimulate damaged areas of the brain with our new technology. We hadn't

115

yet attempted to boost the brain as a whole. We couldn't do that, we thought. We would never get permission to do that, even on comatose patients. Who could guess what the effect would be?

'But we were certainly curious. We would talk excitedly about it late at night. What if we did flood a normal functioning human brain with brain tissue that had been boosted in its capabilities by the introduction of microchips into its chain of DNA? The possibilities seemed endless.

'Too seductive.

'Hapshaw tried it on himself first. The experiment was inevitable, I think, for any true scientist to make. He didn't tell me what he was doing, of course, but I had my suspicions. I guess that's why I wasn't surprised when I came in late one night to work and found his body lying on the floor of our laboratory.'

'What had happened to him?' I asked, finally interrupting.

My grandfather sighed. 'He had shot himself in the head with a revolver.'

I was horrified. 'Why?'

My grandfather shrugged. 'He had left a suicide note. It was only one sentence long. It read: "It's all empty inside." He was referring to what he had seen in his heightened state. I guess Hapshaw didn't enjoy solitude.'

I waited for my grandfather to continue. When he didn't I asked the question I knew he was waiting for me to ask. 'Did you try to boost your own brain?'

'Yes.'

'What happened?'

'Many things.'

'Tell me.'

He sighed again. 'Words cannot explain it.'

'Try. Please?'

He was weary by this time. 'Maybe tomorrow.'

He didn't talk about what had happened until a month later. By then his health was improved and he had gained weight. Once more we were alone late at night in his room.

'I want you to have a clear idea of what I did to myself because it will be impossible for me to give you a precise idea of its effect,' he said. 'I removed cells from my brain with the aid of a special syringe. I then cultured those cells in a test tube so that they lived long enough for me to perform microsurgery on them and tag on millions of molecular computer chips to the DNA of the cells. As you know, DNA controls the functioning of each cell in our body. Essentially, these microchips were telling the DNA to work harder and longer. That's a gross simplification but I cannot say it any better without getting bogged down in complicated GTE terminology.

'I had Hapshaw's own notes to draw from, and although he had ended up committing suicide after experimenting, I wasn't afraid to follow in his footsteps. I believed Hapshaw had killed himself because his glimpse at a higher reality had shattered his expectations, whereas I had no expectations. Did I mention that Hapshaw had been a devout Buddhist? I guess not. To this day I don't know if that mattered. I don't believe that the boosted brain cells had harmed Hapshaw physically. I wouldn't have experimented on myself if I had. I guess I'm saying I believed he went nuts simply because he wasn't strong enough emotionally. I had already been through a lot in life, I thought, especially since your grandmother died. I felt I was strong.

117

'I finally gave myself a shot of the enhanced brain cells. What happened at first was nothing. I went home and enjoyed a perfectly good night's sleep. The only thing different was that I dreamed of my childhood a lot, particularly of one girl I knew – Oh, never mind. I felt just the same is what I want to say.

'But that was to be expected. The cells had to begin to function with my other brain cells and to multiply. That took some time, at least a week. Then I did begin to notice changes in perception.

'Forgive me ahead of time, please. My subsequent experiences will sound like those of someone under the influence of a hallucinogenic drug. I'd be in my lab, eating a cheese sandwich, and I'd notice how incredibly delightful the taste of the cheese was. The texture of the bread in my mouth would absorb my entire attention. Then I would feel the butter as it melted in my mouth and slid down my throat into my belly. I felt as if I could actually see inside my body and know how my individual organs were responding to what I had just taken in. This will sound silly, but it seemed as if each organ in my body – my stomach and gallbladder and liver – had its own feeling about what I was having for lunch. I am saying my entire nervous system became incredibly sensitive. That was only the beginning.

'From that point on, the changes increased dramatically. I began to know things the five senses could not possibly have told me. For example, I would stare at a piece of wood that would steadily expand in my vision, as if I were exploring it under a wide-field microscope. I could detect the actual molecular structures that made up the wood. Now we know that is a physical impossibility. The human eye cannot resolve such tiny dimensions – under any circumstances. At first I assumed I was hallucinating. But then I would have an assistant examine the wood under an electron microscope and he would report back to me the arrangement of molecules that I had already seen.

'Obviously I wasn't seeing these things with my eyes. Another area of perception was at work here. There was now something in me, something in my heightened level of brain functioning, and something in the piece of wood that had connected. I asked myself: could it be that this something had always been there, but I had never had the equipment to detect it? Do you see what I was doing, Sara? I was asking and simultaneously answering one of the original questions that had plagued me throughout my life. This something was *thought*. Somehow my thought was connected to the piece of wood. Yet the wood had no thoughts of its own.'

'I don't understand,' I interrupted.

'I can understand your confusion. This is where words begin to fail. Let me try a different approach. My improved brain was allowing me to see deep into the structure of matter, deeper in fact than modern instruments would allow. The reason was that I was using a more subtle instrument to do my exploring. I was using thought itself. Thought was so refined that it had never been recorded on a photographic plate, never been weighed on a scale, never been measured by a ruler; thought was so delicate that physicists said it didn't even exist.

'Now, to the next question: what was the energy behind thought? It wasn't one of the four basic forces in nature. I decided to regard it as the fifth force of energy. Indeed, I began to consider it the most fundamental energy of them all for it seemed to be in everything. That might sound like a leap of faith, the ravings of an amateur mystic. But consider this: how else was I to explain how I could take a sample of an unknown chemical, study it, *slip* into it, know what

119

it was, and then have that knowledge independently verified? By some strange science, I was *connecting* to the chemicals. I was seeing them without my eyes. I was knowing them without a tool other than my own mind.

'Where was all this going? There was only one direction it could go, to finer and finer levels of matter. I began to spend most of my time sitting with my eyes closed and exploring things around me, going into them, understanding them from the inside out. My research into reality had taken a meditative twist. But I was meditating like no yogi I had ever read about. My thought struck deeper than the most expensive atom smasher ever constructed. I eventually began to perceive the quantum level of matter: neutrons, protons, electrons. I was a walking laboratory. I began to sense mesons and quarks. And I began to know that there was something beneath them all, something that didn't seem to change no matter what. I believed I had discovered the basic material of the universe, the one thing out of which everything else was made.'

'What was it?' I asked.

'Space.'

'But space isn't anything,' I protested.

My grandfather's smile was sad. 'I remembered Hapshaw's suicide note: 'It's all empty inside.' He had come to where I had arrived and it had horrified him. But to me – well, I believed in nothing so I wasn't disappointed that the ultimate element, out of which everything was constructed, was basically nothingness.'

I had to chuckle. 'But that makes no sense.'

My grandfather didn't laugh. 'It is the only thing that makes sense. Beyond the smallest of the small there must be nothing. But let's not debate the philosophical

120

implications of what I am telling you. Suffice it to say that if I had been searching for God I would have been disappointed at finding no one at home when I came knocking.

'Yet I did discover something remarkable in this nothingness. Something my mind could connect with and comprehend – in a limited fashion. I discovered that the universe never forgets anything.'

'What does that mean?' I asked.

'At the finest level, in that space beyond the smallest subatomic particle, the creation remembers everything it has ever been. I use the word *remember* for the sake of simplicity. The pattern of the past is present at every point – in everything.'

'I still don't understand.'

My grandfather leaned forward and rubbed the hair on the top of my head. 'I remember you as a baby girl. Do you know I was there the day you were born?'

'Mother told me. She said it was you who thought up my name.'

My grandfather sat back in his chair. He had been looking better the last few days, but suddenly he seemed old again, ready to quit. He closed his eyes and took a deep breath.

'I gained the ability to look into the past.'

I was astounded. I didn't doubt his words. 'Into all of history?'

'Yes.'

'How far back?'

'All the way back to the beginning of time.'

'You could see it all?'

'Yes.'

'Can you still?'

He nodded weakly. 'Yes.'

'How about the future?'

'The future has not happened. How can the universe remember it?'

'Good question. But, still, you didn't answer mine.'

He opened his eyes and stared at me. I was sitting at his knee, as his faithful student. It was a relationship that couldn't last.

'I discovered I could view many possible futures,' he said. 'The most probable would stand out as a clear line in my awareness. The least likely would hover at the edge – ghosts, tunnels wreathed in fog. I could see these futures, but I couldn't touch them. Do you understand, Sara?'

I nodded. 'The past had more substance because it had once been. The future had none because it might never be.'

'That is correct.'

'What would happen when you viewed the past?'

'Nothing would happen to it. I was not affecting it by viewing it. But the universe would remember perfectly how things had been. I would feel like I was there.'

'Back in time?'

'Yes. I had discovered the only time machine that could be. A key to the memory banks of the universe.'

'Would you be there? Back in time?'

He looked at me strangely. 'You mean, physically? No, of course not.'

'What did you see when you looked into the future?'

He turned away. 'I told you, there are many possible futures.'

I sat up and put my hand on his knees. 'But you said some are more likely than others. What did you see? Was it good? Was it bad?'

His eyes took on a glassy stare for a moment, as if he were looking into the future right then. Whatever he had seen, I knew then it had been too much for him.

'At first what I saw for us, all of us, was tragic,' he said. 'But that didn't surprise me. Man has always been his own worst enemy.' He coughed. 'But maybe I should have left things alone. There are tragedies and there are tragedies.'

'What did you do?'

'Sara,' he said, and there was a note, faint but nevertheless chilling, of despair in his voice. Now, finally, he was scaring me. I clasped his old hands and felt how they trembled.

'What did you do?' I asked softly.

'I wanted to make things better,' he said.

'I understand. Go on.'

'There were going to be more wars – plagues, environmental disasters. I could see it all, in almost every possible future. In fact, there was not a single likely scenario that wasn't choked with misery. Honestly, you can't imagine how awful it was going to be. I had to try to make things better. You can see that, can't you, Sara?'

I sat back on my heels. A chill had come over me that refused to be soothed by the single basement heater. I was so much like him, you see, I could tell which direction he had taken even before he told me.

'You looked into the future and took something from it,' I said.

My insight didn't surprise him or make him feel any better. 'Some technology, yes. I thought if it could be applied at this time, before mankind sank once more into barbarism, great suffering would be averted.'

'What exactly was the technology you sto – took?'

My first choice of word hadn't escaped him. 'I uncovered the blueprint of a thinking machine. A machine that could reason like a human being. A conscious mechanical artifact. The blueprint gave me a direction, so I thought, of where mankind had to head.'

Finally I was getting the big picture. 'In the direction of the robot?' I asked.

'Yes. I had already taken a step along that road when I injected the microchips into my brain.' He shrugged. 'This was merely the next step.'

'Merely? Could you be more specific?'

He could see I was not pleased with how he trivialised such a step, but he accepted that as well because he knew I loved him anyway. I think my love meant a great deal to my grandfather.

'I couldn't build the mechanical brain of the distant future,' he said. 'The technology of that society simply did not exist in our time. But I could do the next best thing. My glimpse into the future had brought me enough knowledge to meld a human nervous system with a mechanical body, a body that could greatly enhance the longevity and the productivity of the nervous system in question.'

'You figured out how to build a cyborg?'

'Yes.'

'Did you build one?' I asked.

'Yes.'

'Using a human nervous system as the basis?'

'Yes.'

'Did it work?'

'All too well.'

'Did this cyborg have your ability to see the past and the future?'

'Yes.' He took a breath. 'And more.'

'What more?' I demanded.

'I could actually go into the past,' my grandfather said. The revelation hung in the air for a few seconds like the blade of a guillotine. But then he closed his eyes, and in the space of a few seconds seemed to doze off in his chair. A half snore wakened him enough to mumble, 'I have to sleep now. I will tell you the rest later.'

I stood up to leave. 'You promise?'

'Yes, Rela.'

I paused. 'What did you call me?'

He was going to sleep where he sat. 'Nothing. Good night, Sara. I love you.'

'I love you, Grandfather.'

We had our last long conversation the following day on top of a hill in the woods, which overlooked the ocean. We had walked there after lunch. The day was sunny and bright and the polluted smell from the ocean was hardly noticeable.

'Tell me more,' I said.

'Finding a usable human nervous system from which to construct the cyborg was the most difficult part,' he said. 'Obviously, I couldn't experiment with a normal healthy person. I had to find someone who was technically brain-dead but whose body was still strong. Of course, working with Hapshaw had given me many contacts with the doctors of comatose patients. But my requirements were even more stringent than they had been when we experimented with boosting damaged areas of people's brains. I was searching for the next to impossible. I needed a patient whose brain had caused his or her death, yet I couldn't work with a brain that was too badly damaged. Because this was the brain I was going to boost a thousand times more than I had my own, and this was the brain I was to place in a body.

'But I must point out at the start that I was taking precautions that my cyborg would never get out of control. I was building it to help humanity. It was to be our ultimate servant. It would be – along with others like it – designed to lead us past future obstacles. It would be able to do this because it would be able to see obstacles in our future. At the core of its programming was the command that it protect humanity from suffering. Just that simple. That instruction was ingrained in every circuit of its memory. When the cyborg was complete and operating it would be impossible for it to run off and cause ruin. That is how I foresaw the matter.

'Eventually I found a young man whose body was being kept alive by mechanical means, but who, for all intents and purposes, had died from a minor stroke in the hypothalamus region of the brain. That is located at the base of the brain, and as you know, the higher functions of thinking are located in the cerebral cortex, relatively far from the hypothalamus. His brain was damaged, true, he was never going to wake up, but EEG readings showed that the majority of his central nervous system was still intact and functioning.'

'What was the man's name?' I asked.

'I never knew. I didn't want to know. He had been in a coma for some time. His family had turned him over to the care of the state. A legal death certificate had been issued in his regard. He was a nonentity and that was the way I chose to think of him. There were a few legal formalities to wade through, but I was eventually given him, what was left of him, to do with what I wished. Before beginning the process of removing the brain and spinal cord from his body, I washed his system with a chemical called THC – theroine hydroxide carbonide. THC counteracts the chemicals in the cells of the brain responsible for memory.'

'You wanted to make sure he had no memory of who he had been?' I asked.

'That's correct. I set to work alone on this momentous task. I did, however, have a team of engineers

126

constructing the cyborg body. They eagerly worked with me because I kept providing them with skills from the future. But once more let me state that we could never have constructed a machine of the complexity of the human brain. I alone had to fuse the brain and spinal cord into what the engineers had built for me. I worked night and day for years, sleeping little. I suppose that shows on my face.'

'Many things show on your face,' I said. 'Many things don't.'

'Eventually my task was complete and the first cyborg awoke. I called him Sam and he was a wonder. He had computer chips, both molecular and standard size, implanted in his brain to stimulate its repair and growth. He had at the core of his system a device that actually generated brain waves. His consciousness was an ocean of perfectly flowing waves. He awoke ignorant, but he awoke with awareness much greater than ours. He learned very quickly.

'Sam looked like a machine. He still does, to this day. But he had more heart than most people I know. I say that in a figurative way because his physical heart was actually a pump that had been built in a laboratory. But I think you know what I mean. It was not long before Sam was talking and walking and busy completing each task I set for him. Immediately he wanted to help me; he wanted to help everybody. But what was he to help me with? The answer was obvious. I had to build a more advanced version of what I had created. I had to make a cyborg that could function in society and not be detected for what it was.'

'Sam had absolutely no memory of any time before?' I asked.

'None. I found another brain to work with, a dead girl this time, and with Sam's help I started work on a second cyborg. I may as well admit something right here. My experiments on myself had greatly enhanced my intelligence, but I was like a child compared to Sam. He built Susan – essentially. I just watched.'

'Susan?' I asked.

'That's what we called her. It was Sam's idea.'

'Sam could have ideas?'

'Yes.'

'He was alive, then,' I said.

'That is what I have been saying all along. He was more alive than you or I. Yet Susan made even Sam look archaic. She looked almost human. Sam had advanced the entire field of skin grafts and tissue regeneration a hundred years. Susan then took over, once she was functional, and made herself even more humanlike. Yet she had Sam's disposition. She was there to serve mankind. How could she help but serve? I had designed her that way. So the process continued.'

'You kept developing new generations of cyborgs, and each one was superior to the previous generation?'

'Yes, except now I had little to do with the process. I couldn't begin to compete with the skills of my creations. Soon I was just overseeing the programme. We were moving ahead quickly. Cyborgs were evolving that were indistinguishable on the outside from humans.

'The shortage of adequate human nervous systems was our biggest obstacle. The cyborgs set out all over the world searching for candidates. Slowly but steadily they built their number up to forty. It was about this time they approached me as a group to found the New Life organisation to help serve humanity.'

'They approached you?' I asked.

'Yes. You are still not seeing them as thinking beings, Sara, but I tell you they can think a million times faster

128

than we. New Life was from the start their creation. I remember laughing when they told me how they would organise and grow and solve the problems of the world. I felt as if all my labours were finally bearing fruit. I gave them my permission to go ahead.'

'They would not go ahead until they got your permission?' I asked.

'Yes.'

'Do they still seek out your permission when making decisions?'

He hesitated 'The answer is complicated. I have to go on.'

'No, tell me now. I have to know who's running the show at New Life. That group keeps growing all the time.'

'Yes,' my grandfather said hastily. 'But the core number of cyborgs is still small. A lot of them are not necessary. You can't have too many leaders or nothing gets done.'

'Who's making the decisions at New Life?' I insisted.

'We are.'

'We? You still have the final say in things?'

'Not exactly. We decide together – sort of.'

'Grandfather!'

'We agree on most issues. There is just one point where we don't see eye to eye.'

'What is that?'

'To answer that, I first have to tell you that when I started on the cyborg project I stopped peering into the future. I didn't have the time, and more importantly, I reasoned that I couldn't look because if I saw that I was to fail, then I'd have to give up before I started. Does that make sense to you?'

'You were worried that the knowledge of your failure would make you fail?'

'Yes. Whether it's true or not, I don't know. I sensed that if each time I used my supernormal abilities to make a decision, then the moment I saw whatever I saw in the future, just that knowledge might distort my decision. I'm sorry. Talk like this always gets complicated because we are dealing with cause and effect, and when you can travel in time it is hard to say when one stops and the other starts. Suffice it to say I had made the decision to give humanity kind guardians and I hoped everything would work out.'

'That sounds weak,' I said.

My remark stung him. 'I just explained why I thought it would be a mistake constantly to check what effect my work was having.'

I spoke carefully. 'Could it have been something else? Could you simply have not wanted to know because you were afraid of failure?'

My grandfather was silent a moment. 'I think I may have been afraid, but of what I'm not sure. In my defence, though, I could see with my own eyes the benefit of what I was doing. From the time Sam and Susan entered my life I recognised a spark in their eyes that could carry a man in directions he'd never have dreamed of taking if he were alone in the universe. Besides, Sam and Susan were monitoring the future and they told me that mankind's future suffering was being all but eliminated by the actions we were taking in the present. I believed them. I had to. They were incapable of lying.'

'Did any of them venture into the past?' I asked. 'You mentioned that last time.'

'Sam did, just once, as an experiment. He returned quickly and we both agreed it was too dangerous to attempt again because we might change something that might affect Sam from ever being created and then he'd cease to be. Then he couldn't have gone back to do what he did and – the circular possibilities were unpredictable. As far as I know, all cyborgs possess the ability to transfer themselves into the past by perfectly accessing the memory of a specific date, the memory of which is stored in the fabric of space, but none of them do it.'

'Essentially they are able to think themselves back in time?'

'That is correct.'

'You are leading up to something, Grandfather. It must have to do with the future. I know you must have peered into it since you took leave of the project. Why don't you just tell me what is going to happen?'

'I didn't want to tell you without first explaining how all this happened. But now that I have done that, I guess it's fair that you know. The main reason I came here was to tell you.'

Time moved slowly for me then. 'What will happen?'

He picked up a stick from the ground. He fiddled with it for a moment before suddenly breaking it in half. 'There are no people in the future any more,' he said.

'*What?*'

'A thousand years from now *Homo sapiens* on this planet will be extinct.'

I was aghast. 'Will the cyborgs wipe us out?'

'No. There will be robots then, not cyborgs as we have today, total thinking machines with no human parts. They will not destroy us, not directly. Rather, we will become them. We will become machines.'

'Willingly?'

'Yes. Or you could say, inevitably.' He stared out at the ocean. 'I made Sam too well. He was programmed to stop human suffering. When he created Susan he gave her the same programming. She in turn gave the next generation of cyborgs similar instructions. When the robots finally walk the earth they will be the great-great-great-grandchildren of Sam and Susan, and they will be our most devoted caretakers. They will work ceaselessly to end every conceivable form of human suffering. There's just one problem with their desire.'

'To be human is to suffer,' I said.

My grandfather looked at me with fresh appreciation. 'You knew that without being told. I only knew that after suffering through everything I have. You amaze me, Sara.'

'More than Sam and Susan?' I asked, and I hated the bitterness that entered my voice. I couldn't help it. My grandfather was a brilliant man, a kind and generous man, but he had gambled with humanity's future without consulting anyone else. He had gambled and lost. He lowered his head and his voice came out low.

'There is nothing to be done,' he said. 'It is too late.'

'That's ridiculous. You said the future has no substance. We can change things. Surely you saw at least one future where mankind existed?'

'No.'

'Even an unlikely future?' I asked, horrified.

'There was not a single one. Not even on the hazy edges of next-to-impossible. I know why. What has been set in motion cannot be stopped. The cyborgs still speak to me. They ask advice. They will do anything I ask of them, except one thing.'

'What is that?'

'They will not destroy themselves. It is not because they have been programmed to protect themselves. They would gladly give their lives to protect humans. They will not destroy themselves because they

132

feel their presence is necessary to help humanity. Do you see? They are too kind.'

'But surely they can see the same future you see?'

'Oh, they do. They see it far more clearly than I.'

'Then they must know they have to leave if we are to survive?'

'Survive how? They do not see our gradual evolution towards mechanical creatures as evil. They see it as necessary, the path of least pain. I tell you, they have our best interests at heart.'

I felt trapped in a nightmare. 'But we will not be who we are. We will be machines. Nobody wants to be a machine. I don't see how we as a race could willingly allow this to happen.'

'Because you cannot see the influence of the cyborgs spread over many centuries, what it will be like to have them working openly in society. I will give you an example. Say you are a student and you have to compete with another student for a position you covet. Now this other student has done what I have done, attached molecular microchips to the DNA of his brain cells. You wouldn't be able to compete with him. He'd be quicker, more imaginative, and his memory would be infallible. But otherwise this other person would seem scarcely different from you. He would still laugh and tell jokes. You would think of him as human and he would be human. In time, you would think, if I am to keep up, I must have the same advantages that he has. You would have your brain boosted, too.'

'No, I wouldn't. I wouldn't make myself even a bit into a machine.'

'I accept the strength of your resolution. But will your children, your grandchildren, be equally resolved? By the time they are older the secret of New Life's organisation will be public knowledge and steadily more and more people will turn to more and more mechanical enhancement to enrich their lives. We haven't even touched upon the most powerful reason to become like a cyborg: they don't age.'

'They're immortal?'

'I wouldn't go that far. They can be destroyed, certainly, if you put them on top of a bomb. They will also, in time, wear out. Yet they will be able to repair themselves. They will be the envy of mortals everywhere. People will want what they've got. People will want to live for ever.'

'But they won't be people if they take that course!'

'Where will the line be drawn? I'm a person, although I have parts inside my head that were made in a laboratory. Few people will have the desire to become a cyborg overnight. But over time, it's inevitable that we will become more mechanised. Mankind will die out.'

'And all this because you created Sam.'

He could hear the accusation in my voice. 'I cannot go back in time and uncreate him.'

'Is there any way of getting them all together and destroying them?'

'No. I've thought of it. They're too smart for that. At best I could destroy a handful of them. They would not retaliate against me even if I took such drastic action, but they would arrange it so that I could not harm them again.'

'There must be a way.'

'There isn't.'

'We can alert the governments of the world! You say their number is small. United, the world can surely defeat them.'

'You underestimate them. They would always be ten steps ahead of us. And I have already explained that nothing *can* work. There are no people in even one

134

of the possible futures I have studied – and I have studied them all. There is no action we can take today or tomorrow or five years hence that will stop what New Life has begun. It is done, for good or bad.'

'How can you say that, for good or bad? There is no good. What you have done is catastrophic. You've wiped out humanity.'

'Who's to say we wouldn't have wiped ourselves out? I tell you, you cannot conceive of the suffering I saw that awaited us as a race. New Life, if nothing else, has spared us that.'

'At the cost of our existence!'

'That's not entirely true. The robots that will evolve from us will carry a part of us inside them. We will live on as a race, but in a different form.'

'You sound like you're happy this has happened.' The bitterness in my voice, fully unleashed, was very unpleasant. My grandfather was wounded by the strength of my reaction, although I can't imagine how else he could have expected me to feel. I mean, we weren't talking about an accidental meltdown of a nuclear reactor or anything small like that.

'I am not happy about it,' he responded quietly. 'I have merely had to accept it.'

'If it is all so set and final, why did you tell me about it?'

He was just an old man then, whose life had not gone in the direction he planned. 'I told you because of something that happened to me as a young man. I knew a girl – we went to high school together. She was a lot like you in many ways. I didn't know her long, but I liked her. Her name was Sara. That was where I came up with your name.' He added, 'Sara died not long after we became friends.'

'How did she die?' I asked.

He scratched his head. 'Her death was never fully explained by the authorities. I'd rather not go into the circumstances surrounding her end, though. They were not pleasant. I brought her up because she, like you, was a great believer in the sanctity of life. We once talked about her views and I think I gave her the impression that I thought she was wrong about the *magic* of life. I never got to correct that misunderstanding before she died. I know in the years to come the truth of New Life will come out and my part in it will become known. I wanted to tell you all of this so you would understand that I did what I did only because I cared for people. I wanted to help protect that magic. I had no other motivation.'

I understood. He could not journey into the past like his creations but he was still living there. Perhaps, I thought, that was why he had recoiled so hard from his first glimpse of humanity's painful future.

I smiled. 'You wanted your Sara to know that?'

He seemed relieved for a moment. 'Yes.'

I lost my smile and stood and patted him on the back. 'The magic is gone for me, Grandfather. It won't be coming back soon.' I turned away. 'I'm going to walk home alone. OK?'

He knew then I would never forgive him for what he had done.

'Fine,' he said miserably.

My grandfather left us soon after that. I spoke to him a few more times over the next year but I wasn't to see him again. Yet he did see me.

For me, the end of the human race was unacceptable. But I had to accept my grandfather's belief that nothing could be done to stop New Life from expanding throughout all society. There was no reason he would have told me so much only to lie to me about what he saw in the future. But there was a possibility my grandfather had not suggested, either because he hadn't thought of it or because he was afraid to pursue it. He could only see the future from where he stood. From that vantage point it looked many different ways, but it was never to be that man would survive.

But what would the future look like from further back in the past?

What would happen if a cyborg went back in time and killed my grandfather when he was a young man?

Without my grandfather there would be no Sam, and without Sam New Life would never have been founded. Yes, it was true that mankind might eventually develop robots, anyway, but the course of the future would have been, even with my grandfather unnaturally out of the picture, closer to what he saw when he first peered into the future. As a race we would suffer, but it would be worth the price to be alive and know that we were human.

I thought so.

Even though it meant my grandfather had to die.

I did still love him, no matter what he had done.

I had only one small problem. I wasn't going to succeed at talking a cyborg into carrying out my plan, even if I happened to meet one. There was only one way around that difficulty.

I had to become a cyborg.

I had to die, but in such a way that when I was revived I still had my memory and wasn't at the whim of Sam's or Susan's programming. THC, the drug that the cyborgs used to wipe out memory, was one of a family of drugs called carbonides. I researched the drugs closely and learned that they could be largely counteracted by a heavy dose of a drug called Nemprin. In other words, if there was a large concentration of Nemprin in a system when the THC was injected, the Nemprin would immediately begin to break it down before it could cross the brain barrier and affect the synapses and neurons. Surprisingly, Nemprin was not a difficult drug to obtain. It was often used in treating depression. I had no trouble getting a purple vial of it.

How was I to kill myself so that my life was not wasted? Obviously my grandfather had to find me just as I died. I could leave him a note, I decided, that expressed my deep desire to be a cyborg. It would be a dying wish and he would fulfil it for me because he would feel so awful for having told me about the cyborgs in the first place.

Plus the cyborgs needed fresh brains to make new children. I did more research and learned that a drug named Cyclomone would kill me by destroying select areas of my brain that had little to do with higher brain functioning. Cyclomone was not an easy drug to obtain, but after long effort, I had a green vial of it to match my purple vial.

I flew to New York City. That was where New Life was centred and that was where my grandfather had returned. Incredible, I thought, after all he had told me, he had gone back to them. But I knew why.

My grandfather was a coward.

Pain frightened him. Well, it didn't frighten me. I would destroy myself to destroy them and I would do it with a willing heart.

Yet it was easy to talk that way – until it came time to stick the needles in. Then I was afraid. I kept thinking of all the things that could go wrong. What if they checked and flushed the Nemprin out of my system before they hit me with the THC? Then I would be just another happy member of the New Life council.

I kept thinking of how young I was.

I didn't want to die.

When I arrived in New York, I called my grandfather and agreed to meet him for lunch. New York was a mess that day. They were having a zone nine smog alert and breathing outdoors was almost impossible. My grandfather sounded happier than he had been on the hill overlooking the ocean. He must have believed I had come to patch up our differences. I had come to kill us both.

He was to pick me up at one o'clock in my hotel room. I had my vials with me, and a bathtub filled with bags of ice to keep my remains cool. My syringes were new, and I tore off their plastic wrappers as I removed them from my purse. I had a piece of paper by my bed and a pen with which to write my suicide note. I wanted to put down something for my mother and father to read, but I knew they'd never see it if my grandfather respected my last wish. Plus they'd never understand why I'd had to make such a sacrifice.

You might think me noble or maybe crazy. I suppose a person cannot be truly one without the other. My plan was bold, but it would succeed only if I was willing to commit murder. I could see that my grandfather was old, that he had already led an interesting life, and that he couldn't live much longer. But when I saw him again as a young man would I have the strength to lift a knife to him? There was only one way to prepare myself for such a trial. I had first to lift a knife to myself.

It was a quarter to one when I started to write my note. My grandfather had always been fanatically punctual but seldom early.

The phone rang. I lifted it. 'Yes?'

'I'm down in the lobby,' he said. 'Are you ready? Can I come up?'

'I need time,' I said softly. He noticed something in my voice.

'What is it?' he asked.

He could know only that I wanted to be a cyborg, not one who thought it was a teenage girl. I was not going to be writing him a note.

'I'll be dead in a minute,' I said.

He gasped. 'Sara? Don't do anything. I'm coming right up.'

'Don't put down the phone,' I snapped back. 'My syringe is already filled.' I put emphasis on the singular. 'I have Cyclomone. One hundred ccs – a lethal dose.'

His silence was filled with shock. 'But why?' he croaked.

'You said it yourself. There are people who just want to live for ever. I'm one of those. Make me one of those – a cyborg. That's all I want. If you won't, you'll just have to bury me and then it will be like you never had a favourite little girl.'

'But, Sara!' he cried in anguish. 'You can't do this.'

'You don't know what I am capable of doing, Grandfather.' I slammed down the phone and stabbed my syringe into the vial of Nemprin. The purple fluid went down easy. My veins drank it up. I noticed no immediate effects from the drug. Quickly I took the empty vial, the syringe and the syringe wrapper and threw them out of the fortieth-storey window.

Then I picked up the green Cyclomone.

I took hold of the second syringe. Stabbed the vial.

'Forgive me, God,' I whispered.

Stabbed my arm. The Cyclomone burned.

I heard footsteps running up the hall.

I fell back on to the bed and stared at the ceiling.

It looked so far away.

Someone began to pound frantically on the door.

I closed my eyes. I died.
For the first time.

What happened then was better told in my nightmares.
The dreams of the dead. I floated for ever until I was
dumped in an icy bath. Then they, the cyborgs, came for
me and put me in the mechanical chair lit by the orange
light, the chair that could change into an upright bed,
and have the back removed so that the cold hands and
whining blade could cut into my spine.

How could it have been so terrifying, what they did
to me when I was dead? I don't know any more than
I know what the word *dead* means. My brain wasn't
working while they operated on me, but a part of me
was there. A part of me would remember.

Maybe it was my soul.

But poor Sara was not the rebel cyborg she had hoped
she'd be when her nervous system was finally fused into
a robot's body. Perhaps the Nemprin didn't work as
well as it was supposed to. Perhaps some of the THC
crossed the brain barrier before it could be broken
down into its component parts and made harmless.
In either case, I was a zombie when I woke up. And I
stayed that way, largely, until I remembered the purple
vial. Then, at least, I had the strength to think myself
back into the past, into that city and time where the
great Professor Christopher Perry was a young man.
But I didn't have the heart to bring back my memory,
and I think I was wrong to condemn my grandfather
so quickly for being a coward. Because I don't think
my amnesia had as much to do with the drugs as
it had to do with the fact that I didn't want to die
and I didn't want to kill.

That was the crux of my problem when I material-
ised on the streets of Pasadena in my hospital gown.

I had died wanting to save the world and I had died wanting to have a chance to live the life of a teenage girl. Which desire was stronger? When I recovered my senses I plunged into being a normal girl. I went to school, I ate cookies and milk, and I wrote secret love letters to a boyfriend. Yet I chose my boyfriend carefully, without being aware of it.

I chose the young man I had come to assassinate.

What about the VCR? It was just a vehicle that allowed me to tap into my true abilities. In my cyborg mind I could reach into the data banks of the cosmos and pull out anything I needed to know.

I could do it in my sleep. I could impress the information on the tape with one of my silver fingers. No problem.

It had been my subconscious that had been telling me what still needed to be done. Unfortunately I had had to go and save the window washer, and upset time in such a way that the cyborgs of the future could locate me before I completed my mission.

I had screwed it up. It was a pity.

But it wasn't over yet.

I still had to kill Christopher – if he gave me the chance.

FOURTEEN

'Yes, Grandfather,' I said. 'It was you who named me.'

He did not pull the trigger on his weapon. My remark appeared to interest him. 'You know who I am?' he asked.

'Yes. You were always afraid of pain. You went back to New Life because you knew your days as a mortal were ending. You were afraid to face that end. You probably took the Nemprin, like I did, before you let the cyborgs put the THC into your veins. I bet you faked them out. Then, as time went on and the technology of your offspring improved, you made yourself more and more mechanical until you finally became the perfect thinking machine you had originally glimpsed in the future.' I paused. 'You have brought yourself back in time from more than a thousand years from now.'

'Your analysis is correct. I am from the year 3116. In a sense I am your grandfather. I have all his memories. But I am much more than he ever was.'

'Then why don't you pull the trigger?'

'There is time,' he said simply.

'You have another reason for delaying. You don't want to kill me.'

'I assure you I will destroy you momentarily and that I will feel no discomfort when I do so.'

I sneered. 'So you are the crowning achievement of humanity. A complex computer without a drop of humanity in it. What happened to your precious programming? How can you kill me? You are supposed to protect me.'

'Technically you are already dead. I am under no obligation to keep you alive. Also, you have to be destroyed so that billions of humans will not suffer the future you are trying to recreate by killing Christopher Perry as a young man.'

'You can kill one to save billions? The end justifies the means?'

'I have already stated that technically you are already dead.'

I glanced at Christopher. He was so close, so vulnerable, but I knew I would not be able to reach him before the robot cut me down. I had ten times the strength of a normal human being, but I suspected the robot had ten times that. I was not going to win by acting rashly. I gestured to Christopher.

'What are you going to do with him?' I asked.

'He will wake up tomorrow morning in his own bed. He will remember everything that happened until the moment he blacked out. He will hear about your death when he calls your foster father here in the morning. The incident will disturb him for years to come but he will get on with his life and complete the work he was meant to do.'

'He was not meant to create a cyborg,' I protested. 'He stole the information from the future to build it.'

'He obtained the information for the good of humanity.'

I had to laugh. 'The good of humanity? Gimme a break. Your kind will wipe out humanity. How can you possibly justify your existence as being for people's benefit?'

'I am unmoved by discussions of this kind. It will

not prevent me from destroying you. Sara once said to be human was to suffer. I am opposed to all suffering. I will answer your other questions – why I am delaying shooting. I have qualities of humanity in my make-up. For example, I share your grandfather's curiosity. He was curious about all things. I have a couple of questions I want to ask you.'

'You didn't want to ask them until I called you Grandfather.'

'That is correct.'

'Why?'

'Let us say your calling me that stimulated my ancient curiosity. May I ask my questions now?'

'When I am through answering them you are going to shoot me?'

'That is correct.'

I blinked. 'I should take my time answering them. Shoot – I mean, go ahead, ask your questions.'

'Why did Sara put herself through pain and suffering to try to alter the future by going into the past?'

'To save the human race.'

'But her saving the human race, in the form she wished to save it in, would have caused more pain and suffering to more people?'

'Is that your second question?'

'It is a third.'

'OK. Just let me know when you're coming up on the last one. My answer to you is, so what? From my perspective and the perspective of most humans it is better to be alive and suffering than not to exist.'

'But we are not discussing non-existence. I exist. Humanity survives through us.'

'But that's my point. You are not human. By the year 3116 you will have destroyed the very things that make us human.'

'You are a cyborg; you are no longer human.'

'But I am human! I have feelings! I have a soul! Even when you cut my spine and brain from my body, I survived. I am Sara, damn you. I am not Rela.'

'You have the memories of Sara. But Sara killed herself. Once a human dies he or she stays dead. That is a scientific fact.'

I felt beaten. 'Are you dead, Grandfather?'

'Yes.'

'Then why don't you just shoot me and get it over with?'

'I need to ask my last question. Once Sara told her grandfather, after he explained the origin of New Life to her, that she believed not all suffering was bad. That good could come from it. I would like you to expand upon that comment.'

'If I give you a really great answer will you spare me?'

'No, but your answer will give me a certain satisfaction.'

'How do you know that?'

'All your answers do.'

I sighed. I was capable of the gesture. 'All right, I will answer your question. I told my grandfather that if there was no suffering in the world, there would be no compassion.'

'That comment is in my data banks. Please continue.'

My eyes were suddenly damp. I understood what was in the black suitcase the robot had brought. It was human tissue to replace the artificial tissue I had in my body so that the police wouldn't become suspicious when an autopsy was performed on me. That was the reason the robot had to mutilate me completely, so that my true nature would not be uncovered.

146

'I told my grandfather that,' I said. 'But I also wanted to tell him that I loved him.'

'Sara told him that many times. It is in—'

'Your data banks, yeah, I know. But your data banks are lacking in a few areas. I died before I could make it clear to my grandfather that I forgave him for his mistake. Love can do that for humans. Love often brings the most pain of all, but it also brings the most joy. Can you understand that, Grandfather?'

I expected the robot to deny that he was my grandfather. But he didn't. He just stared at me. He still had the weapon pointed at my head, but something had changed in his eyes, perhaps; they were softer, warmer.

Maybe it was my imagination.

'Are you going to destroy me now?' I asked.

'Yes.' He moved the weapon closer. 'Goodbye, Sara.'

Someone knocked at the front door.

FIFTEEN

The robot paused. The person knocked again.

'May I answer it?' I asked.

'Will you tell whoever is there who I am?'

'I seriously doubt if they would believe me if I did.'

'Answer my question.'

'If I do tell them, what will you do?'

'In all probability I will have to destroy them as well as you.'

'You can kill a living human being?'

'I can kill if it is necessary to stop the suffering of billions of other humans.

'It is simple maths to you?'

'Yes. Will you tell whoever is there who I am?'

'No. Not if you are going to kill them.'

He removed the weapon from my head and slipped it into his back pocket. 'You may answer the door after I have lifted Christopher on to the couch. You will act like I am a friend and that Christopher is sleeping. You will get rid of whoever is there as fast as possible without appearing strained. Do you understand?'

'If I don't do these things it is more likely you will kill whoever is at the door?'

'That is correct.'

'I'll do what you say. May I get up now?'

'Yes.'

The robot was fast on his feet. He had Christopher

resting comfortably on the couch, his feet dangling near the VCR – which was still on the coffee table – before I could round my chair. He had removed the tape from the VCR, the one that chronicled my death, before I could open the door.

'Hi! Has the bogeyman come for you?' Ed asked, giggling beside Stacy on the front porch. They didn't look especially relieved to see me alive. I glanced at my watch. It was only a quarter to ten. A lot had happened in the last few minutes. I had relived an entire lifetime.

'I thought you couldn't get off until ten?' I said to Ed.

'You sounded so upset, I just closed up,' he said. 'Then I went to Denny's and you weren't there. You had me worried, Rela, I have to tell you. I called Stacy and told her what was happening and she thought we should come here. The two of us drove up together.'

'Is a man really following you?' Stacy asked.

'Yes. Sort of.' I glanced over at the robot. 'But it's a long story. I'm safe now. Christopher's here. He's asleep on the couch. He's had a hard day.'

'Is this man a psycho or what?' Stacy asked, sticking her nose further in the door. 'Hey, who's that guy?'

I had to act natural. If I didn't, I had no doubt the robot would strike quickly, 'Just an old friend,' I said and forced a laugh. 'His name is Hal. Hal, come over and I'll introduce you to Ed and Stacy.'

'Let us come in,' Ed said, barging past me. 'It's chilly out here.' He stuck his hand out to the robot. 'You're Hal? Pleased to meet you. The name's Edward, but everybody calls me Ed except my mother. I'm a friend of Rela's.'

The robot smiled warmly and shook Ed's hand. 'It's a pleasure to meet you, Ed,' he said sincerely.

149

'Wow, where did you get that tracksuit?' Stacy asked the robot.

'Nordstrom's,' the robot said. 'On sale. You're Stacy?'

The robot had not used contractions in his speech until Ed and Stacy had entered the house. Of course, there had been no reason for him to try to act human around me. The robot and Stacy shook hands and introduced themselves. Stacy was not as silly as she acted, as I have often said.

'Where are you from, Hal?' she asked, and there was a suspicious note in her voice. After all, a strange man had supposedly been following her best friend. Now here was such a man. It was a shame her concern could get her killed.

'New York,' the robot said smoothly. 'I am just here for the evening. I am friends with Reverend Lindquist.'

'Is that so?' Stacy asked, giving me an inquisitive look. She was searching for signs of anxiety in me and I was determined to show none. It was easier now that I knew I was a cyborg to control such things. On the outside at least.

'Hal will be spending the night,' I said smoothly. 'He just got here. I'd have liked to offer him the couch but I don't know what to do with this fella here.' I gestured to Christopher and giggled. I was a bit puzzled why the gas in the house wasn't getting to Stacy and Ed as well, but then I remembered the robot had said it would dissipate quickly. I could only assume that Christopher had inhaled a fair dose of the gas and that it was still working on his nervous system. 'He just lay down before Hal got here and passed right out,' I said.

'Weird how all this talking is not waking him

150

up,' Ed observed.

'He's a heavy sleeper,' I said.

'How do you know?' Stacy wanted to know.

I smiled. 'A girlfriend knows these things.'

'I want to wake him,' Stacy said, stepping towards the couch. I stepped in her path. 'Rela?' she asked.

'Why do you want to wake him?' I asked. 'Let him sleep.'

'I want to talk to him,' she insisted.

'He's tired,' I said. 'Please, just leave him. You can see he's breathing comfortably.'

'Hey, there's that amazing machine I sold you,' Ed broke in, pointing to the coffee table. 'Were you taking it somewhere, Rela?'

'Yeah. Over to Christopher's.'

'I heard he can fix VCRs,' Ed said.

'He can fix just about anything,' I said.

'You left your *Lethal Weapon* tape here, Stacy,' Ed said. He had found it leaning against a magazine rack not far from the coffee table. He got all excited. 'Hey, I've got to show Rela Mel Gibson's butt in slow motion. I swear to you, Stacy, Rela only got the four heads because she wanted to enjoy dirty films to the max. You should have seen her mouth watering when I described how she would be able to slow down the – Oh, I'm sorry, Hal, I forgot you were standing there for a second. Please forgive us. We're just crazy California kids, you know. All we talk about is sex and the ozone layer.'

Hal smiled politely. 'Two important topics, to be sure.'

'Hey, that's cool,' Ed exclaimed. 'To be sure.' He picked up the VCR along with the *Lethal Weapon* tape and took a step towards the TV. 'I'm sure you won't mind, Hal, if I plug this thing in quick and show Rela the special features she spent her hard-earned cash to get.'

'Ed,' I said, beginning to feel desperate. The robot was giving me looks. He wanted them out of the house soon, or else he was going to take matters into his own hands. 'Another time might be better.'

'Hell,' Ed said, already fiddling with the electrical cords at the back of the TV. 'There's a shot of this woman on this tape I can show Hal. Don't be so uptight, Rela. He's from New York. They vote Democrat there.'

Stacy still wasn't sure about Hal. 'What part of New York are you from?' she asked him.

'Manhattan,' the robot said. 'I work in the computer industry for a small software firm called Comp Complete. We specialise in operating systems for old IBM mainframes that can't take the new operating systems but whose operating efficiency can be improved by taking codes from parts of the new and blending it with code from the old. The firm has been in business approximately five years and has clients in Los Angeles. I am primarily here on a business trip.'

'Oh,' Stacy said. He was so smooth. I watched as her suspicions visibly evaporated. I was thankful and I was crushed. I would be dead that much sooner.

Except for maybe Ed. He already had the VCR plugged in and was sticking in the tape. He was about to turn on the TV when the robot interrupted.

'To be honest, Ed,' the robot said. 'I am tired from my travels and don't think I am in the best state to enjoy a video right now. Would it be possible for us to watch it another time? I would like to retire for the evening shortly.'

'Huh?' Ed said, the remote control in his hand. 'Oh, yeah, that would be fine.'

'Hal is very tired,' I said, stepping over to Ed. I took the remote control from his hand and turned my back to the VCR, shielding it from the rest of the room. The robot had removed the tape of the news from the machine, that was true, but I could feel the movie tape still in place. I had been hiding my robotic ring finger from Stacy and Ed simply by keeping the fingers of my left hand clasped. Now, going by feel alone, I pulled the cable free that normally went into the TV and stuck my peeled finger into it. I remembered my late night excursions then. This was how I had been impressing the next day's news on the tapes. The robot was preoccupied with Ed. Ed was telling Hal about a prostitute he once met who was from New York. I pressed the Power button on the VCR with my right elbow.

I began to record this story. At high speed.

The story of Rela and Sara.

'Stacy, Ed,' I said, interrupting Ed's ravings. 'You guys go out and have fun. Leave us sleepyheads alone.'

'Is that what you want?' Stacy asked, serious.

Ed glanced round at Christopher sprawled on the couch, Hal standing perfectly still, and me leaning on the VCR and TV as if I were too tired to stand up on my own.

'I think that's what they want,' Ed said.

'It is,' I agreed.

Stacy came over and gave me a brief hug. I patted her with my free right hand. Stacy's eyes had never looked so kind.

'Call me first thing in the morning, you hear?' she said.

'I will,' I promised. I kissed her on the cheek. 'You are my friend.'

Stacy grinned and rolled her eyes like a fool. 'You

153

better believe it, babe.' She kissed me quickly. 'Good night, Rela.'

'Good night to both of you,' I said sadly. They bid Hal a fine evening and left through the front door.

But Ed slammed the door as he left.

The robot looked over at me.

He began to pull out his ray gun.

But the noise had disturbed Christopher.

My boyfriend, Grandfather, opened his eyes and looked around.

'Where am I?' he asked.

SIXTEEN

The robot motioned for me to remain where I was. I had to, if I wanted to stay plugged in to the VCR and continue to record my story. In this very moment, I record this very moment. I am fairly certain I'll be dead in a few minutes. That's why I said what I did at the beginning, only a minute past as cyborgs measure time. But nothing is definite yet. If I can get my hands on Christopher, and kill him – and I can break his neck as easily as if it were made of straw – then the robot will cease to exist because Christopher will never become him. And I will cease to exist because Christopher will never have my mother as a daughter, and she will never have me as a daughter. Then the room will be empty, except for Christopher's dead body, and the news, the second news, will be on TV tomorrow night as scheduled.

Christopher sat up and looked around.

'Rela?' he mumbled groggily. But then his eyes fell on the robot and he sat up straighter. 'Who are you?' he asked.

The robot looked remarkably like an older version of Christopher in his photograph. But in person, with his weird grey cat eyes, the resemblance faded. It struck me then that my grandfather had spoken of meeting me, Sara, when he was in high school. Yet when I was still human, still his granddaughter, he had not recognised me as the young woman he had known as a kid. I suppose the cyborgs had not gone out of their way when they constructed my body to make me look identical to my stunning original, although from my memories of Sara I knew a resemblance was still there.

So I had come back before. Or maybe this was the before. Maybe it was just one big circle of time where cause and effect chased each other like cats after their own tails. But if that was so, I had already failed and couldn't win.

Yet I had discussed that exact point with my grandfather. It was possible that simply the knowledge that one time-line of Rela had failed could allow me to be victorious. In either case, I knew what I had to do.

I had to kill Christopher.

For mankind. I had to keep telling myself that.

'My name is Hal,' the robot said smoothly. 'I am a friend of Rela's father. I'm from New York.'

Christopher looked at me. No doubt he was thinking about the strange man who had supposedly been chasing me. The situation was curious. I knew the robot didn't want to take overt action in front of Christopher because he wanted to affect the course of his life as little as possible. Frying my guts with a laser pistol a few feet away from the budding young scientist would not be at the top of the robot's agenda. I realised I could force a scene. But something made me wait. You understand I say *made* instead of *makes* for the sake of the continuity of form in my story. I am waiting now. Christopher is fidgeting on the couch.

'Is that true, Rela?' he asked.

'Yes,' I said. 'Hal and my father have been friends for a long time. You don't need to stay. Hal will be spending the night. I'll be perfectly safe.'

'But you were anxious to leave a minute ago,' Christopher said.

'I overreact at times.'

Christopher frowned. 'Wait a second – I fainted. Did you see me faint?'

'Yes,' I said. 'You work too hard. You need to rest. You should go home to bed. Really, I'm OK.'

'But I've never fainted in my life,' Christopher said, slowly getting to his feet. 'I don't understand it. How long have you been here, Hal?'

'I just arrived,' the robot said. 'You were asleep on the couch. I didn't know you had fainted.'

This robot sure could lie, I thought. But Christopher was staring at him, and I remembered how perceptive he could be. He had to sense that there was something different about Hal.

'What kind of work are you in, Hal?' Christopher asked.

'I work in the computer industry for a small software firm called Comp Complete. We specialise in operating systems for old IBM mainframes that can't take the new operating systems but whose operating efficiency can be improved by taking code from parts of the new and blending it with code from the old. The firm has been in business approximately five years and has clients in Los Angeles. I am primarily here on a business trip.'

It was word for word the same answer he had given Stacy. It seemed to put Christopher at ease as well. He smiled. 'You have the right name for being in the computer industry,' he said.

'Christopher is referring to the computer in *2001: A Space Odyssey*,' I said.

'I know the movie,' the robot said.

'Hal went nuts and killed most of the human crew,' I said, staring at the robot. 'He had lousy programming.'

'That would never happen in real life,' the robot said, staring back at me. He didn't know what I'd do next.

157

Christopher took a step past the robot, moving closer to me. I continued to hang on to the VCR cord.

'I guess I should be going if you feel everything's all right,' said Christopher.

'Everything's fine,' I said. 'I'll see you at school tomorrow.'

Christopher grinned. 'Hopefully after school. You know you owe me a date. You stood me up on Tuesday.'

'I'm sorry. I promise I'll make it up to you later.'

Christopher looked over at Hal, then back at me. 'Do you want me to walk out, Rela?'

The robot shook his head faintly. There was still plenty of time left to throw my scene. But once more I hesitated. Christopher only had to come five feet closer, I thought, and I'd be able to snap his neck.

'It's cold outside,' I said. 'Why don't you just kiss me goodbye here?'

My boldness surprised Christopher, but he was obviously shy about kissing me in front of a stranger. I felt nothing incestuous in the suggestion. The body I was in now had nothing to do with the body his daughter had given birth to. Only the brain and spinal cord were the same. The lips were different. Plus I wasn't going to kiss him. I was going to rub his neck. I was going to press my fingers deep between his cervicals until I heard a distinct snapping . . .

Silently I began to weep inside.

It was for everybody, I told myself. The whole planet.

Christopher took a step closer. He was almost in range.

I couldn't fail. I had sacrificed my life to succeed.

'Are you going to bed right away?' he asked.

'Yes.' I glanced at the robot. 'I'll sleep. It's been a while since I really rested.'

Christopher also threw the robot another look. He was obviously trying to give him a nonverbal suggestion that he wanted to be alone with me for a minute. But the robot, of course, wouldn't allow that.

'So when do you want to get together?' Christopher asked me.

'Tomorrow night would be good.'

'What time?'

'Any time is good.' I added, 'Any time with you is good.'

Christopher took another step closer. He was close enough to grab now. Behind Christopher, on my right, the robot put his hand in his back pocket. My body shielded my left hand from the robot. My right hand was free. If I lashed out with it, a single karate chop to the neck would crush Christopher's spinal cord. He would die instantly. There would be no pain for him. I could give back humanity's pain. I could give back their life by taking just this one life.

But I couldn't do it.

I felt my eyes moisten.

Some cyborg – I couldn't find the switch to turn off the tears.

Christopher put his left hand on my shoulder.

'What's the matter?' he asked, worried.

Behind Christopher, the robot withdrew his ray gun and pointed it at my head. But he was a few feet away. I had Christopher practically in my hands. It would be a test of reflexes but I believed I could win. At the very least I could pull Christopher into the line of fire.

But I loved him – my grandfather. I had treated him with scorn for what he had done, but I had never stopped looking up to him.

I couldn't do it.

I had to do it.

'I just hate to see you go,' I said, taking his hand with my free hand. My tears were flowing now. I was the one bawling, but Christopher's hand felt so fragile in mine. It was only flesh and blood. It could suffer pain. I was not supposed to know pain any more. Yet it was all I knew in that moment.

I knew then what I had told the robot was true.

I was human. I had survived. My soul, it was real.

Christopher touched my face. 'But I will see you tomorrow, Rela.'

'Sara.'

'What?'

'My real name is Sara.'

'Why have you been going by Rela?'

I grinned like a silly sad fool. 'It's a long story. Maybe sometime I can tell you. But call me Sara. Say, "Goodbye, Sara. You're a great girl."'

'You're great,' he told me, and he hugged me. I snuggled my head into his shoulder, and watched as the robot lowered the weapon. He knew I could now do to Christopher what I wished and he would not be able to stop me. I held on to Christopher with my free hand, but I didn't touch him with the other. I ran my hand up his spine to his neck. My fingers pressed into his skin there and he seemed to sigh. He was tense and I knew I could relax him – permanently.

But once more, I couldn't do it. I had killed myself, but I could not kill another. It wasn't because of some cyborg programming. It was just me. I wasn't strong enough.

'I love you,' I whispered in his ear. The human race would die because of my love. He squeezed me tighter.

'I love you,' he said. Then he let me go and brushed a tear off my cheek. 'You take care of yourself, Sara,' he said.

I let him go. 'I will,' I promised.

'We'll have fun tomorrow night.'

'It will be wonderful.' I patted his shoulder. 'Remember.'

He was puzzled. 'Remember what?'

'Remember the butterflies and the trees.'

He grinned at my sentimentality. 'And Sara.'

I smiled. 'Most of all Sara.' I swallowed. 'Goodbye.'

'Goodbye,' he said.

Christopher said so long to the robot and left the house. I watched him go. I watched the bright flame of the future leave to burn a scar across the path of human destiny.

'You could have killed him,' the robot said when we were alone.

'Yes.'

'That was your purpose in coming back.'

'Yes.'

'Why did you not try to complete your mission?'

'Because I have something inside me greater than anything you have.' I stared at the robot. 'The future you come from is nothing.'

'We are highly advanced. We want for nothing.'

'Because you have nothing.'

'I have no more questions for you.' He took the weapon from his pocket and pointed it at me. 'It will be better if you move away from the TV.'

'You think you've won,' I said.

'I have won. You have lost. You will be destroyed now.'

'He'll remember me.'

'That is understood. I remember you.'

'But you don't know me. He knows me.'

'It will make no difference. New Life will happen.'

I didn't have time to sit and peer into the future,

although I had the ability to do so. But a feeling suddenly swept over me from seemingly nowhere. It sweeps over me now. I don't know exactly what it is, but there is hope in it. Not hope for today or tomorrow or even a thousand years from now, but hope nevertheless, that life will go on, and find something greater than a mechanised grave. In a sense I want the same thing that my grandfather wanted, that people should not suffer. Yet I am not like him. He remade himself so that he could live for eternity. Yet he never defeated the eternal enemy – no, not the cyborgs or the robots. The enemy is fear, simple fear. Grandfather was always afraid of suffering.

I am not afraid. I want something more for people. I want them to be happy, and I believe our suffering as a race can eventually bring us to a place of great wonder. For all I have suffered since I came back in time, I have been happy to be alive.

'It will make a big difference,' I whisper.

The robot shakes his weapon. 'Move.'

I have died before.

No one should mourn this, my second death.

I begin to remove my finger from the VCR cable.

'Where do you wish me to stand?' I ask the robot.

EPILOGUE

Rela had been dead a month when her foster father came over to Christopher's house with the VCR under his arm. At the time Christopher was alone, working in his bedroom on a programme he believed would boost the sensitivity of his biofeedback machine twofold. He heard the knock, though, and met Rela's father at the door and invited him inside. The minister sat on the sofa, resting the VCR on his lap, and Christopher sat on a nearby chair. He offered Rela's father something to drink but the man said he was fine.

'I don't have a lot of time to spare,' the man said. 'But I wanted to stop by to say hi. We haven't talked since the funeral.'

'I haven't talked to many people since the funeral,' Christopher said.

Reverend Lindquist nodded sympathetically. 'Nor have I. But I have others to care for and, as they say, life goes on.' He coughed suddenly as if he didn't truly believe his words. He removed a handkerchief from his pocket and dabbed his forehead before continuing. 'It's hard to imagine she's gone. I wake up in the morning and keep expecting to see her at the table, eating her Cheerios. She loved Cheerios in the morning, with lots of milk on them.' He shrugged. 'But she's never there.'

'I miss her,' Christopher said.

Reverend Lindquist studied him closely. 'I see that. You only knew her a short time but she got to you, too, didn't she? She was a remarkable girl. There was something different about her.'

'I only wish I'd known her better,' Christopher said. He didn't know what else to say. Words did nothing to soothe his grief. It had not eased during the past month. It had only got worse. He doubted it would ever truly be gone.

'I'm sorry,' the minister said. 'I'm intruding on your pain, when I . . .' His words trailed off and his eyes moistened. He lowered his head. 'It's just that I have so much myself, I guess I want to share it.'

Christopher leaned forward and touched the man on the knee. 'Don't apologise. She loved you a great deal. Any time you want to talk about her, please come over.'

He looked up. 'Did you know I was only her foster father?'

'Yes. She told me.'

'I only knew her three months.'

'I didn't realise it was that short a time.'

Reverend Lindquist nodded. 'Three months. She was like a shooting star in my life. Bright, beautiful – and then gone so quickly.'

'The police still don't know anything?'

Rela's father shook his head sadly. 'Nothing. Your description of that man, Hal, has led them nowhere.' He stopped himself before he was taken over by his sorrow. He patted the VCR. 'The main reason I came by was to give you this. Rela bought it just before she died.' He set it on the sofa beside him. 'I never watch tapes myself. I thought she'd want you to have it.'

'That's very kind of you,' Christopher said.

Reverend Lindquist spoke suddenly. 'Rela had twenty-one thousand dollars in her chest of drawers.'

Christopher sat up with a start. 'Really? Do you know where she got it?'

'No.'

'Did you tell the police?'

'Yes.' The man shrugged. 'It didn't help. They told me to keep it. I plan to give it to the mission.' He added, 'If that's OK with you?'

'I don't want any money,' Christopher said.

'I thought as much.' The older man stood. 'Well, I'd better be going. I have to be at the mission in half an hour. Did you know that's where I met Rela?'

'I didn't know that either.'

'A man brought her in from the street. She only had on a green hospital gown. Can you imagine? She was wandering around in a daze. We never did find her real family.' He dabbed at his face again with his handkerchief. 'I'm certainly not trying to find them now.'

'You were good to her.'

The man's hurt was like an open wound. 'I should have taken better care of her.'

'It wasn't your fault. It happened. What can you do?'

Reverend Lindquist shook his head. 'I'm the minister here. I should be saying those things.' He patted Christopher on the back. 'Hope to see you again soon, young man. Enjoy the VCR. Rela had to save to buy it.'

Christopher didn't tell the minister Rela's correct name. Let her father remember her as he knew her, he thought. 'I might use it today,' he said.

Christopher had not really meant he'd use it. He had a VCR of his own and it was a better one than Rela's. But when the minister was gone Christopher carried the VCR into his bedroom and set it on his desk. On impulse he plugged it into his TV. He noticed there was a tape already in the machine – the first *Lethal Weapon*.

He had no desire to see the movie again, but rewound the tape as a matter of habit. He was turning back to his programme for his biofeedback machine when he accidentally bumped the VCR Play button with his elbow.

Maybe it was fate.

Rela's face sprang on to the screen. Sara. She was talking.

She was in the middle of telling a story.

No, she was in the middle of *her* story.

He could see her on the tape, doing the things she was describing, in full living colour. He didn't understand how this could be. He had never seen a tape before so rich in definition. And her voice – it sounded as if she were right there in the room with him.

Christopher hit the Stop button and hastily rewound the tape to start it at the beginning.

'I was just a normal teenage girl. I loved beautiful clothes and loud music, long telephone conversations and sleepy summer evenings. Most of all I loved cookies and boys. My favourite cookies were chocolate chip – with milk. You've got to have milk to have cookies. That's what I always said.

My favourite boys – well, actually, I had only one favourite boy. His name was Christopher. My name is Rela . . .'

Christopher finished watching the tape two hours later. He scooted back from his desk and turned off both the TV and the VCR. Night had fallen by then, but he left the light off. He often thought best sitting alone in the dark.

He believed the tape was accurate. The fact that it existed was proof enough. Also, he wasted no time wrestling with the wonder of it. He had been dreaming about the origin of the universe since he was ten. He wasn't surprised that it was his fate one day to discover it. He had always known he was a man of destiny.

But what did he know? What was he supposed to learn in the years to come? It appeared an immensity, yet he had been struck, while watching the tape, by how much better Rela had understood what was important in life than her grandfather. That man comprehended the universe. She knew people. He might be the new Einstein. She had been – she would be – special.

I knew her, he thought. I will know her. And she was right, at the end. I already see her in a light her grandfather never did. I will remember her as she wanted me to, and perhaps the circle of mankind's time will be healed.

He was grateful the tape had stopped before she died.

He hadn't liked the robot.

'I will never become that thing,' Christopher said with bitterness in his voice, but also with resolve. 'Never.'

If you have enjoyed THE ETERNAL
ENEMY, you might also like other
books by Christopher Pike published
by Hodder and Stoughton

Coming soon . . .

by

Christopher Pike

Here is the first chapter . . .

ONE

My sleep, as our plane neared Greece, changed, but I cannot say how. I would like to say that a dream, a vision maybe, entered my unconscious state and filled me with wonder and fear. But if this happened I cannot remember it. I do know I *sensed* the approach of this ancient land before I awoke. I sensed it in the same way a child senses home, and awakens, just before the parents pull the car into the driveway. The stir in my sleep was familiar. I was coming home – to a place I had never been before.

Then I heard the captain's voice announcing that we had begun our descent. I opened my eyes and was momentarily blinded by the morning light, a morning that had never come so swiftly for me before. The flight attendants had pulled up the window shades. Yawning, stretching, I glanced over at Helen Demeter. She was already wide awake and staring at me.

'Are we there yet?' I asked.

'Fifteen minutes,' Helen said

'How long have I been asleep?'

'Hours. You snore.'

'I don't snore,' I said quickly.

'It must have been the soul that occupies your body while you sleep that snores,' Helen replied.

My mouth tasted like the last thing I had eaten before I passed out, which I think was old peanuts. I sat up straighter, heard my neck crack, and swore to myself that I must be getting old. I was stiff as a corpse.

'Do we get breakfast?' I asked.

'We just had breakfast,' Helen said.

'Why didn't you wake me?'

'You didn't look hungry.' Helen made a face. 'You need a breath mint, Josie.'

'I need and shave and a shower,' I said – and my name is Josie Goodwin, and I'm a girl.

'Brush your teeth and ask a flight attendant for some orange juice. He might take pity on you. The Swiss are very polite.'

We were flying Swissair, nonstop from L.A. to Athens. Helen and I were in coach, my father and his new babe, Sylvia – or 'Silk', as she preferred to be called – up front in first class, where they could stretch their legs as far as they wished. Not only were their seats as big as ones at home, but all the champagne they wanted was on the house. I wondered if Daddy and Silk were stewed. He was drinking more since he'd met his latest. My dad was a Hollywood screenwriter. He was one of the best. I didn't know what Silk was other than a pain in the ass.

'All right,' I said, grabbing my carry-on bag and lurching to my feet. 'Don't let anybody take my seat.'

'It's not as though you can wait outside until we land,' Helen called after me.

My skin was the colour of wet plaster in the bathroom mirror. My blonde hair was matted to my head. The veins in my eyes were the colour of whisky. And I was supposed to be pretty – really, somebody somewhere had told me that. I think it was my last boyfriend – Ralph. I had really liked him, Ralphy Boy. So had Helen, for that matter. But Ralph had moved away, and Helen and I were still friends.

I brushed my teeth and washed my face. Then I used the toilet, and that thing almost took off my butt when I flushed it. Incredible suction – I could have believed I was on the Space Shuttle. As I left the lavatory I asked a flight attendant if I could have a hit of orange juice, and he handed me a cup, made me drink it on the spot, and then he told me to get in my seat. But the blue ocean, incredibly gorgeous in the first morning light, still looked a mile below us, so I rambled up to the first class to see my dad.

He was sharing a joke with redheaded Silk. Outside of Hollywood, they would be an unlikely pair. Dad had balding grey hair that had failed to respond to transplants and rolls of fat that were immune to fad diets – he was a battered fifty. Silk must have passed her mid-thirties, although she was still striving to be ready for her teenage auditions. Her face was great, but hard somehow. Her firm chin may have been an implant. Her green eyes were definitely contacts. But that hair – I had to grant that Silk had hair worthy of her nickname. It flowed all the way down to her butt, which had ridden the most expensive bicycles in Beverly Hills.

But in Hollywood such couples were natural. An out-of-work actress of questionable talent latching on to an out-of-work screenwriter of immense talent. Who was hoping for more? Daddy or Silky? In their own sad way they did fit together.

Sad for me.

'Hi, guys,' I said, interrupting their chuckles. 'Did you miss me?'

'Josie,' Dad said. 'We checked on you an hour ago and you were out for the count.'

'You were snoring like a pig,' Silk said.

I gave the sweetest smile. 'At least I get it out of my system when I'm asleep,' I told her.

'Jo,' Dad muttered.

'Daddy,' I said innocently.

But I hadn't insulted Silk, because she was too stupid to realise it. Or maybe I was wrong about that. Sometimes, when I was feeling paranoid, I wondered if Silk took in everything and simply filed it away for future reference, when her position was stronger.

'I cannot rest for a moment on a plane without my blue bomber,' was all Silk said.

'What the hell is that?' I asked.

'A sleeping pill,' my dad said dryly. 'Be grateful you slept, Josie. We're getting in early. You'll be ready for the sun and the water and we'll be in bed.' He looked tired. 'At least I got some writing done.'

'Did you?' I asked hopefully. My father always brought his laptop computer when he travelled, but he seldom did anything more on it than write letters. He was currently doodling on a sci-fi script that he hoped would put him back on the studio executive lunch circuit. But he had writer's block – no, it was more like writer's wall, writer's mountain, writer's black hole. He hadn't had an original idea in the past year. His drinking wasn't making the situation any better. That was another reason I disliked Silk. She was under the erroneous belief that booze got the juices flowing.

My father nodded to the laptop resting on his lap and chuckled grimly. 'I signed on, put in the date and time, and reread my notes.'

'I touched his shoulder. 'The word *muse* is Greek. Maybe one of them is still hovering around the islands and will drop in and pay you a visit.'

He looked up at me. 'You're the only muse I need.'

His compliment had a grain of truth in it. I often helped my father with story ideas. I had a knack for it.

The plane shook beneath my feet. I almost fell into Daddy and Silk's laps.

'Better sit down, dear,' Silk said. 'We wouldn't want

you to get hurt before your vacation begins.'

'I'd rather not get hurt on my vacation either,' I said, like the snotty little girl I could be. Saying 'See you soon,' I turned and hurried back to my seat. Once there, Helen helped me fasten my seat belt.

'I didn't tell you that the Athens airport is the foulest place on the face of the Earth,' Helen said. She had visited Greece the year before. Indeed, it was largely because she raved about her vacation that we were all going now. 'They hate Americans with a passion. They'll spit on you the moment you get off the plane.'

'But the pamphlets say the Greek people are warm and friendly,' I protested.

'They're not so bad on the islands. But the airport is bizarre. Terrorists hold weekly meetings there. They sell plastique in the restrooms. You can be shot for saying, "Hey Zeus".'

'What?'

'"Jesus". That's "Hey Zeus" in Spanish. Plus the food is lousy,' she added.

'Well, we won't be there long.'

'We have to take a cab to another airport to catch our plane to Mykonos,' Helen continued. 'The cab drivers hate Americans. If you don't tip them enough they drive you back to Athens airport and tell the people there that they didn't spit on you enough.'

'You are exaggerating a tiny bit. I can tell.'

Helen shook her head. 'It is all very true.' She returned to her book – a travel guide to Mykonos and Delos. Like she was the one who needed to read it and not me. The plane shook some more. Over the speakers the captain said that we would be on the ground in three minutes and that the flight attendants should sit down.

'Tell me more about the nude beaches on Mykonos,' I said.

Helen lit up. She was pretty when she smiled. Her hair was brown, a no-nonsense short cut, her small nose cute, something to squeeze if you were into such things. She was slight – two inches shorter than my five five – but not bony. I thought she was pretty, but even though I had known her for ever, I didn't know what *she* thought. She had a talent for many things: singing, dancing, homework, art. Yet I got asked out more often, even though all I could do was help my dad with his stories.

When Helen wasn't smiling, she looked like she wasn't happy. But she would laugh when I told her that, and I would be reassured.

'The nude beaches are combined with several of the regular beaches,' Helen said. 'Not everyone is naked – maybe half. But few women wear tops.' Helen paused. 'Are you going to wear your top?'

'When my dad's around, yeah,' I said. 'But I'll take it off if he's not there. I'm not that shy. But I don't think I want to go totally nude. Are you going to?'

Helen hesitated. 'If you don't, I won't.'

'Are there a lot of gorgeous guys?'

'You mean, are there a lot of gorgeous body parts?'

'Yeah.' I laughed. 'Certain body parts?'

Helen nodded. 'Yeah.'

I rubbed my hands together. 'I love vacations.'

I was not a virgin, nor were Helen and Ralphy Boy. Oh, I say that so flippantly. It was not a kinky threesome – at least, not in one time frame. But Ralph Frost would certainly remember Josie Goodwin and Helen Demeter in the years to come – although maybe not in that order, since he'd gone out with Helen first. But I can honestly say I didn't steal Ralph from Helen. He had broken up with her before he asked me out. Of course, I could have said no. That's what friends are for, I know, to say no when it matters, as often as they say yes. But I didn't, then or later, when Ralph worked his seductive charm on me and we did it on the floor of his bedroom beside his huge aquarium and his bug-eyed fish. Nowadays it was hard for me to think of sex without remembering those fish. Helen, I suppose, must have the same problem.

Anyway, I think I broke Helen's heart a little for being with Ralph, and I was sorry for that. It was kind of a relief when Ralph moved away. Yet I didn't understand why he had never written to me – not a single letter, not even a card. I really did care for him. Oh well, I tried to console myself, Helen mattered more.

A few minutes later the plane landed smoothly, and when it came to a halt everyone jumped up at once as if they were going to be the first off. Helen and I were patient. I stacked my books back in my carry-on bag. I was currently into courtroom thrillers and was thinking of becoming a lawyer. Helen and I had graduated from high school a month earlier, in June. But with that thought I was being practical, because what I really wanted was to be a screenwriter like my father. The problem was, even though I was wonderful at thinking up stories, I didn't have the discipline to sit down and write anything. I couldn't even complete a letter. I wondered if Ralph hadn't written because I had never written to him.

Eventually we got off the plane. Customs was a joke. They didn't even look at our passports – just saw we were Americans and waved us through. No one even glanced at our bags. And Helen had lectured us on how strict they were.

The airport was hot and sweaty and crowded. We each changed some money. I had my own; it wasn't courtesy of my dad. I worked with a caterer twenty hours a week. The official currency of Greece was the drachma. Right then we got a hundred and sixty of them for a dollar. I changed two hundred U.S. dollars, and with the wad they handed me in return I felt rich. Helen was anxious to get us over to the other airport to make our connection to Mykonos. Helen was always neurotic about time.

No one spat on us, but no one smiled either. We left the airport, our bags piled in a couple of rental carts, and got in a long line to catch a cab. The sun was intense and I began to perspire. The buildings in the vicinity were dirty. I couldn't complain – I was from L.A.

'It's cooler on Mykonos,' Helen said as I wiped my forehead.

'That's good,' I said. 'How long is the flight there?'

'A half hour,' Helen said.

'Will there be someone to meet us at the airport?' Silk asked. She had dressed up for the trip – always a mistake. Her purple dress and coat were close to being ruined. She had brought more bags than the rest of us combined. Helen and I were dressed casually in khaki shorts. Dad had on a pair of pants he should have thrown out the year before. He had to unbutton them to sit down.

'It's questionable,' he said.

'Oh, Bill, didn't you make sure?' Silk asked, a whiny tone to her voice. Silk had a habit of whining when she was tired and if she didn't get her daily nap, which was supposed to be at about five o'clock. I hated whiners.

'I faxed the people at the hotel a number of times, honey,' Dad said. 'They said they'd do what they could. We can always catch a cab.'

'The cab drivers on Mykonos are all crazy,' Helen told Silk. 'They hate redheads with a passion. They think they're witches.'

'Oh, dear,' Silk said.

We finally got a cab. The driver drove like a madman. I supposed I would have done the same if I had to wait in line at the airport several times a day – it would have driven me nuts. He took us straight to Olympic Airlines. At the terminal I had to help with Silk's luggage – we all had to. I handled her bag roughly; it felt as if it was stuffed with back issues of *Cosmopolitan*, maybe an X-rated video or two. We groped our way inside, out of the heat and into an oven, and still no one spat on us. Helen looked disappointed when I pointed the fact out to her.

The flight to Mykonos was in forty minutes. I amused myself by sitting on the floor – all the seats were taken – and reading my latest thriller. The hero was about to find out that the woman he was defending had not only actually committed the murder but had cheated on the bar exam as well when the two of them had taken it twenty years earlier. Spicy stuff. I glanced over at my father as he typed in a few words on his laptop and gave him a wink. He smiled – he knew he wasn't going to write more than a useless sentence or two in a crowded airport.

At last we were on the plane, a two-engine prop job that I hoped had been built in the U.S. Inside, before takeoff, it was a thousand degrees, and it warmed my heart to see Silk on the verge of passing out. But the air-conditioning came on once we were in the air. I sat in the back of the plane beside Helen. She peered out the window.

'I have always dreamed of renting a sailboat and sailing out from island to island,' she said, almost with a sigh. 'Wouldn't that be heaven?'

'It does sound wonderful,' I said. 'Maybe we can do it when we get older – and learn to sail.'

'Sailing around these islands is not always that easy. There's a wind that comes up around Mykonos called the *meltémi*. One second the water is flat and calm and the next it's churning. The *meltémi* will probably kick in a time or two while we're here.'

Half an hour later we were at Mykonos. We had to walk from the plane to the terminal. The airport was small; there were no pushing crowds. The surrounding terrain was rocky, hilly – what tourists thought all Greek islands were. Yet even though it was arid, it was beautiful. I liked it immediately. Athens had not been as horrible as Helen had described, but there had been a certain heaviness to the place. Mykonos was the opposite. There was a feeling of life in the air, of fun, of adventure. Indeed, I suddenly felt as if I had reached an important crossroads in my life. I knew this would be a trip to remember for a long time.

There was a gentleman waiting for us – Mr Ghris Politopulos. At first I assumed he was a hired hand at the hotel where we were staying, but he was both the owner and the manager of the place. His face was fascinating, thick-lipped with a warm smile and the palest, coldest blue eyes I had ever seen – one of which was lazy, rolling this way and that as he scanned our luggage.

'Welcome to Mykonos,' he said in heavily accented English. 'You will love it here. But this' – he gestured to our bags – 'you don't need so many clothes here. Mykonos is always warm this time of year.'

'I have many of your father's things in my bags,' Silk said to us, annoyed at the hired help questioning what she'd brought.

'Do our rooms have ocean views?' Helen asked Mr Politopulos.

'One of the rooms does,' he replied.

Helen flashed a glance my way and we shrugged in unison. We both knew which room would be ours, and that was fine. Helen's parents had paid for her plane ticket, but my father was shouldering the hotel bills. Helen's trip was a present from my father to me.

We boarded Mr Politopulos's van and headed for the

178

hotel. Mykonos was not big, only ten miles across, and soon we were bouncing our way along the outskirts of Hora – the main city on the island. Mr Politopulos explained the colourful history of Hora. Egyptians, Phoenicians, Cretans, and Ionians had all lived on the island in the B.C.s. Turks and an endless train of pirates had run the place later – the population would explode, then become almost extinct depending on which way the winds of war were blowing. It wasn't until the 1950s that tourism took hold and island life began to resemble what it was today. At that Mr Politopulos laughed, saying that Mykonos was basically a big party island. He had been born on Mykonos and had lived his whole life there.

We never entered Hora, however, but turned south away from the city for the remainder of the ride to our hotel. It was only then I got my first good look at the sea, and I was in love. The water was a jewel blue the Californian coast would never know, the sand clean and uncluttered, lazily draped with brown bodies of enviable shape and elusive covering. Already I could see several pairs of male buns and I knew I would have a crick in my neck long before the vacation was over.

Helen pointed to an island out at sea, perhaps five miles away. 'That's Delos,' she said. 'The most sacred island in the Aegean Sea.'

'Why is it so sacred?' I asked.

'Because Apollo and his sister Artemis were born there,' she said.

The sun flashed in my eyes as I stared at the island. I had to close them briefly, and once more I had that sense of coming home that I had had on the plane. I felt I had been to this place before.

'I want to go there soon,' I whispered.

'We'll go there tomorrow,' Helen said, watching me. Our hotel was simple, with white-washed walls built to withstand the heat and sun. It was well situated beside a beach, but close enough to town so that we could walk in at night for the party life. Mr Politopulos checked us in and showed us our rooms, helping us with our bags. Dad and Silk's suite was spacious and on the second storey overlooking the surf. Mr Politopulos warned us to watch the doors and windows when the wind was blowing.

'A man last week got struck on the head by a window and he had to be taken to the hospital for stitches,' he said. 'The *meltémi* – it blows fiercely when the gods are in the mood.'

'The gods,' I muttered. 'Does anyone in Greece worship the ancient deities?'

Mr Politopulos smiled, his lazy eye staring at my rubber sandals, his other one regarding my face. 'Not worship,' he said. 'But many still respect them.'

Our room was on the ground floor, in the back. It had a view of sorts. It overlooked the corner of the swimming pool, where, by golly, there were a lot of naked females enjoying the sun. We had narrow twin beds and a bathtub that looked as if it had been designed for a race of dwarfs. Neither of us believed we would be spending that much time in our room.

'Are you tired?' I asked Helen. Her brown eyes were bloodshot.

'A little. But if I sleep now I'll never get on the schedule here.' She stowed her cheap suitcase in the corner. Her family didn't have much money, even though it seemed as if they must because their only daughter had gone to Greece twice in a year. Her parents were anxious to keep her happy – for various reasons. Of course my dad was running low on funds as well. He had to sell something soon, even if it was only a movie-of-the-week or a sitcom pilot.

180

'Do you want to go into town and walk around?' I asked.

'No, we can do that after the sun goes down. That's when the action starts. Let's go snorkeling, but not here. The beaches on the other side of the island are much nicer – there are Agrari and Paradise.' Helen rolled her eyes. 'Lots of naked bodies on those beaches.'

'How do we get there?' I asked. 'Can we take a bus?'

'Maybe, but we don't want to. The best way to get around is on a motorbike. We can rent them outside of town for less than fifteen bucks a day. Have you ever ridden a motorbike?'

'No, but I'm game.' I had seen couples on the bikes on the way to the hotel and it looked like fun.

'You have to learn how to shift gears. No one wears a helmet here. It can be dangerous.'

'If you did it, I can do it,' I said.

Helen was amused at my confidence. 'We'll see,' she said.

We changed into fresh shorts and T-shirts and bade my father and Silk goodbye. They were already half asleep. Hora was ten minutes on foot. Walking into town along a bumpy asphalt road, we passed what looked like a worthy beach. I still couldn't get over how clear the water was. But Helen reassured me that the beach was nothing compared to what we would see on our motorbikes.

The surrounding houses were all white, dazzling in the sunlight, their balconies festooned with glorious geraniums and pots of basil. Closer to the city, the houses grew thicker together, and I could see that one facade blended into the next, with narrow flagstone alleys winding between them. Helen stopped at a bike shop at the edge of this wonderful town.

She was familiar with the bikes, and I suspected she

had used the place on her previous trip. A pleasant young Greek woman with spotty English helped us pick out bikes – two new Hondas. She demonstrated how to shift the gears, kicking successively down with the left foot. It didn't look hard, but Helen warned me that I would need practice to get the hang of it.

'Wait till you're going uphill,' she said. 'Then you'll have fun.'

Helen's prophecy came to rapid fruition. Our bikes were low on fuel, the Greek woman warned us. We had to go straight to the gas station, and by luck the place was straight up the hill from the shop. I got the bike going well enough and was out on the road, but I quickly lost speed as the incline steepened. Helen was in front of me, pulling away, as cars and other motorbikes roared past me. I thought I was in first gear, the best one for a steep hill, but I must have been in second. I kicked the gear lever, and still I continued to slow down. The bike slowed to the point that it was in danger of falling over. Then it stalled. I coasted over to the side and dug my sandals into the asphalt. The bike was trying to roll back down the hill.

'Damn,' I said.

The scooters had kick starters. I fiddled with the gears before giving it a kick and discovered I had been using third gear. Using the heel of my left foot – the front of the foot upped the gears, the heel lowered them – ground myself back to what I hoped was neutral and then, with my right foot, gave the starter pedal a good swipe. Apparently I wasn't aggressive enough. Starting a bike is a real macho thing, I realised. Putting a slight sneer on my lips, as if I were James Dean, and gritting my teeth, I gave the pedal a real he-man slap. It roared to life.

I rode all the way up the hill in first gear. I was taking

no chances on stalling out. Helen was waiting for me at the gas station, a smug expression on her face.

'Having trouble?' she asked.

'Not at all.' I swung my leg off the bike, feeling cool.

Helen nodded to the pump. 'One full tank will last us three days. I told you, this is the way to get around. Just don't crack your skull on the pavement and we'll have a blast.'

We gassed up and were soon on our way to Paradise Beach. Helen had decided on that one. The road continued to rise for half a mile. Soon we were treated to a glorious view of the western side of the island. Then the city was behind us and we were in the back country – if it could be called that. The silhouettes of windmills on the hills were a reminder of days gone by. There was so much grey rock, its domain broken only by the many white chapels, raised on outcroppings so forbidding I wouldn't have wanted to approach them on a windy day. I counted eight churches in the space of a mile. I had read a bit about them in Helen's travel book. Apparently prosperous sailors long ago were fond of erecting them before going on a dangerous sea voyage. The hope was to gain divine protection.

The road was bumpy and hilly, but I could have been a Hell's Angel in a past life. My mastery of the shifting gears came with a few minutes of experimentation. I do believe it was a look of shock on Helen's face when I came roaring by her at thirty-five miles an hour. The warm air and the brilliant sunlight were a delight on my face and bare arms. The blue coast of the other side of the island came into view. My laughter must have rung in Helen's ear as I passed her. Suddenly I realised I was on vacation and having the time of my life.

A few miles later a splintered wooden sign pointed the way to Paradise, to the right, off the main road. By this time Helen had drawn abreast, warning me not to get too cocky. Together we turned on to the gravel road that led down to the beach. I wore sunglasses, as did Helen, but the rays of the sun sparkled on the water like igniting jewels, and occasionally I had to shield my eyes. It was an odd thought to have, but it was hard to believe it was the same sun in the sky that had shone on me all my life in L.A. I remembered that in Greek mythology Apollo was associated with the sun.

We parked and locked our bikes and sauntered down to the beach. Near the sea the mass of grey rock turned to golden sand before being covered by crystal blue waters. There were no waves – who needed them? The sea was various shades of cerulean, changing colour with the depth. The sand was lighter in colour than the California brand, but grainier. There were beautiful people everywhere, and only half of them had bathing suits on. I liked to look – who doesn't? And I had never before had so many young men to stare at. I can honestly say, without a shred of shame, that I didn't miss Ralphy Boy one bit right then.

'We should have grown up here,' Helen said.

'We should move here,' I replied. 'Who needs college.'

'You can see why I wanted to come back.'

'I can't see why you left.'

We had towels that we'd borrowed from the hotel. We didn't have snorkeling equipment, however, or sunscreen. I had frequented the beach since school had let out and had a good tan. Indeed, I never burned, no matter how long I lay out. But Helen had a problem. It was a priority to get her fair skin firmly shielded behind sunblock, thirty or better.

We took care of the screen for Helen in a small store and were directed to a stand farther down the beach that was supposed to rent masks, fins, and snorkels. All at once Helen was not anxious to get in the water. She said she wanted a drink and pulled me towards the bar, located at the rear of the beach under a thatched roof.

'There was this guy from England who worked here last summer,' she said. 'He said he'd be back this summer.'

'Is he the reason we're at this beach?'

'It's a nice beach.'

'I understand,' I said.

'His name's Tom Brine. We went out a couple of times.' She added unnecessarily, 'I liked him.'

'Maybe he has a friend,' I said hopefully. I wasn't looking for a quick vacation romance, I told myself. On the other hand I wasn't swearing off one, either, which was, I thought, the best attitude.

The bar was crowded. There was no sign of Tom. A shade subdued, Helen ordered a beer, and I did likewise, after a moment's hesitation to note that they weren't asking for I.D. I didn't drink a lot, even at parties, because I invariably woke up with a headache. But I had to watch Helen when it came to booze. She had a tendency to do things to excess. We turned our backs to the bar and sipped our beers, enjoying the view.

'He could be here this summer but taking the day off,' I ventured.

'I didn't expect to find him,' Helen said quickly, lying.

'What was he like?'

'Funny. Smart.' She added, perhaps in reference to the Ralph episode, 'You would have liked him.'

'Was he cute?'

'Who?' a voice asked behind us.

We turned in unison and Helen's face broke into a big grin. I didn't have to ask. Tom Brine was a cutie.

His face was pale, typical of many English young men. He seemed to be scholarly in a way with alert green eyes and messy brown hair that the sun was swiftly turning the colour of the sand. He was thin but in good shape and stood remarkably straight, as if at attention. I put his height at six feet, maybe an inch more. He was a couple of years older than we were.

'Tom, do you remember me?' Helen asked.

He scratched his head. 'You're from America, right?'

'Yeah,' Helen said, a little worried. The lifeguard on duty would have known we were from America.

'You were here last summer?' Tom continued.

'Yeah,' Helen said.

Tom gave a sly smile. 'You break into wicked Italian while in the heat of making passionate love?'

Helen hit him playfully. 'That girl came earlier in the summer! I know you remember me. You look too happy to see me.'

Tom snapped his fingers suddenly. 'Melon!'

'Helen!'

'We went out once,' Tom said. It seemed to come to him all at once and give him pleasure.

'Twice.' Helen leaned her elbows on the bar. I hadn't seen her so excited in a long time. 'You had the time of your life.'

'Was I sober?' he asked.

'Most of the time,' Helen said. 'How have you been, Tom? Oh, this is my friend, Josie. Josie, meet Tom. He's from England.'

Tom was quick to shake my hand. He gave me the once-over but was subtle about it – I only knew from his eyes. His accent was a delight. I had always thought English accents sounded cultured.

'Josie,' he said. 'You are definitely from California and you definitely know Italian.'

186

'Just the naughty words,' I said.

He laughed and nodded to my beer. 'How's your drink keeping?'

I took a gulp from the bottle – some German brew. 'Great.'

'Hey, I'm here for a week,' Helen said. 'When do you get off work?'

'When the sun goes down,' Tom said. He had been drying glasses as he spoke. He had big hands, skilful fingers. 'I'd love to get together with you ladies later.'

'I don't know if you could handle two of us at once,' Helen said, her smile forced. 'Do you have a friend for Josie? She's just getting over a heartbreaking affair.'

'That I've already forgotten,' I murmured. She might have been talking about Ralph, I think, or she might have simply been talking.

'There's Pascal,' Tom said. 'Do you remember him? Big? French?'

'I'm not sure,' Helen said.

'You may not have met him,' Tom said. 'His English is only fair.' Tom looked at me. 'But the ladies all like him.'

'The ladies might not have the same taste as I do,' I said.

Helen and Tom narrowed down when and where they would meet. I felt hot from the ride in the sun and I was anxious to get in the water. Yet – and I am a horrible friend – I liked Tom. He seemed like a nice guy. Of course, they all do at first.

We said our goodbyes and went for snorkel equipment. Helen asked me what I thought of him.

'He's cool,' I said. 'I hope his friend is as nice. But big, French, and can't speak English – what are you getting me into?'

'We'll have fun,' Helen assured me.

The snorkel equipment was inexpensive: the whole works for eight dollars a day. We told them we wanted it for three. Helen used her credit card this time. I had put mine down when we rented the bikes. We could figure out who owed what later. Neither of us was picky about money.

The water was warm, clean, colourful – I couldn't get over how much I loved it. With our equipment on, we paddled out to a number of docked sailboats and then swam over to the jetty. I swear, we were in fifty feet of water and I could see the eyes of the fish on the bottom eating from the long grasses that grew up from the sand. There was no coral, but plenty of interesting stone. I had a fantasy as I snorkeled that I would suddenly spot a gleam of buried treasure. But it was just a dream.

The fish, of course, made me feel kind of horny.

We had been snorkeling for close to an hour when I suddenly felt a pain in my chest. It started in the centre and quickly spread in a band across my ribs. The pain was frightening, but not totally unexpected. I was overdoing it. Ten months earlier, at the end of the previous summer, I'd had a bout with pericarditis, which is an inflammation of the sac surrounding the heart. It can hit with varying degrees of intensity. My illness had been particularly severe. I was hospitalised for three weeks, ten days of which I spent in intensive care. The disease hit with incredible speed and had at first mystified the doctors. By the time I was diagnosed, I was close to death. My fever was so high I lay in semi-conscious slumber for days, knowing little, except that I was in pain, horrible pain every time I took a breath.

Yet after the illness I had been happy, for it seemed that by coming so close to death I had gained a new appreciation for life. The simplest things that I had taken for granted, such as walking to school in the morning or eating ice cream, now came to have special meaning for me. I had also decided to take my future more seriously and buckled down with my studies. My grades my senior year had reflected my newfound dedication. I got almost straight As.

The doctors believed I had made a full recovery, without permanent damage to my heart, but they had warned that my endurance would only return gradually. Even now, so many months later, I was aware that I was not at full strength.

The pain hit me when I was near the end of the jetty, a quarter mile out. I briefly contemplated trying to climb on to the rocks and resting, but there were waves, battering the jetty hard enough to knock me down if I tried to stand up, and the rocks were covered with moss that looked slippery. Helen was fifty yards off to my right, swimming around a huge yacht. I debated calling out to her but was embarrassed. I know it was foolish. Helen was my old friend. My problem was genuine. I was having trouble breathing; I was on the verge of cramping. But I hated to appear weak, particularly in front of her. The aversion had started the previous summer, after my illness.

Slowly I began to swim towards the beach. How quickly my perceptions could change. Moments before the beach had looked within arm's reach. Now it was miles away. I cautioned myself to take my time, to breathe slowly and deeply. At first the strategy worked. I was halfway in and looking good. But then all at once I tired. The pain in my chest returned like a hammer pounding. The muscles in my legs knotted and stiffened. I had been saving my arms – every good snorkeler knew the arms couldn't compete with the fins. Panic entered my mind. Could I actually drown in front of five hundred sunbathers, on my first day of vacation? The thought sent a shot of cold terror up my spine. I began to thrash with my arms, trying to pull myself to shore as fast as possible.

It was the worst thing I could have done. In a minute I was exhausted and gasping for air. I pulled my head out of the water and took my mouth off the snorkel – another mistake. It was easy, while snorkeling, just to relax in the water, facedown, and not even paddle at all. But all I could think of was getting to shore.

I accidentally took in a mouthful of water and coughed. Now I was eagerly searching for help and I wouldn't have minded if it came from Saddam Hussein. But I was at the end of the beach. The sole lifeguard was in the middle, and he had plenty of naked women to look at on the shore, and I think he was asleep anyway. I didn't glance behind me, to see if Helen was nearby. I didn't want to turn away from the beach for even a second because I feared I might move a foot away from it.

I couldn't swim properly with my head out of the water, But I was too shaken to replace my snorkel and put my face back down. The pain in my chest was like the heat from a torch blowing blue flame through the lobes of my lungs. Honestly, I thought I was going to have a heart attack. The smell of the hospital came back to me then, the vapour of rubbing alcohol, the beep of the monitors in intensive care. It seemed that beep had been the first thing I heard when I had awakened from my long burning dream, a mechanical pulse in my ears, some bloodless heartthrob. *Beep, beep, beep* – you're alive, little girl. But it seemed there had been a pause – I suddenly remembered this – a short one, when the beeps had stopped, and there had been silence . . .

I felt myself sinking.

Nothing but the silent roar of cold air blowing through a wide empty space. Yes, I remembered, the beep had definitely stopped.

'Josie!' a voice spoke in my ear.

A strong arm yanked my head up.

I blinked – I must have closed my eyes.

'God,' I gasped.

It was Tom.

The shore was still a hundred yards away. Tom was swimming in place beside me. He still had his work shirt on. How he had got there didn't matter, not to me. His arms were round my waist, lifting my mouth and nose out of the water.

'Just relax,' he said, slipping behind me, moving his arm under my arms. 'Relax into me, Josie. I'll tow you in.'

'I'm all right,' I said, coughing.

'The hell you are.'

We were in shallow water a couple of minutes later. Tom helped me remove my fins and took my mask and snorkel. He held me by the arm while I staggered on to the beach. There I collapsed on the sand, grateful for the chance to catch my breath. I was not having a heart attack. The pain in my chest began to diminish. In the space of five minutes I was almost fully recovered and terribly embarrassed. Helen came running out of the water and stopped beside Tom, staring down at me.

'What happened to you?' Helen asked.

'Nothing,' I muttered.

'I think she cramped up,' Tom said.

Helen was amazed. 'And you came to her rescue?'

Tom shrugged. His shirt was dripping wet, along with his shorts. 'I was watching the two of you from my place at the bar. I noticed Josie having trouble.'

'Why didn't you call me for help?' Helen asked me.

'I got a little tired is all,' I muttered. 'I didn't need to be rescued.'

Helen knelt by my side, taking my hand. She spoke

to Tom. 'Josie was in the hospital last year. It's easy for her to overdo it. She has a bad heart. She—'

'I do not have a bad heart,' I interrupted angrily. My humiliation was deepening. I forced a smile and shook off Helen's hand. 'Don't talk about me like I'm an invalid.' I glanced up at Tom. 'I'm OK, I would have been OK. But I want to thank you for your concern anyway.'

Tom nodded. He understood I didn't want a big deal made of the matter. 'I'd better get back to my job. They're not paying me to be a lifeguard.'

Helen stood up and touched his chest. 'Thank you for saving my friend, Tom,' she said sweetly but seriously.

'Oh, brother,' I mumbled, my eyes rolling.

'I didn't mind a cool dip,' Tom said.

'See you tonight,' Helen said. She raised up on her toes and kissed his cheek. Tom nodded and turned to leave. Helen knelt beside me once more.

'Are you really all right?' she asked.

I sat up and sighed. 'Yes.'

'What happened?'

'Nothing.'

'Why didn't you at least act grateful to Tom for saving your life?'

'My life was not in danger!' I snapped. Then I quietened down. 'I got tired is all. I don't like this being made into a big production.'

Helen nodded, studying me. 'You embarrass easily, Josie.'

I returned her stare. 'So do you, Helen.' I added, 'Let's not talk about this with my dad. It'll only make him worry.'

'I understand,' Helen said.

'Good.' I got up. 'Let's get out of here. Too many people are staring at me.'